SOUL TRAITOR

TIM CHIZMAR

PRAISE FOR TIM CHIZMAR

"Reaches past the conventions of the commonplace"

— CLIVE BARKER, MASTER OF HORROR AND THE
CREATOR OF HELLRAISER, LORD OF ILLUSIONS,
NIGHTBREED, CANDYMAN, ETC.

"I knew I had a long-lost horror loving cousin somewhere out there in the world...and I think I just found him. Tim Chizmar -- what?! No relation, you say?! -- is now on my short list of new authors to look for! His stories are bizarre and scary and sizzle with raw energy. Check him out!"

— RICHARD CHIZMAR, EDITOR AT CEMETERY DANCE
MAGAZINE AND THE CO-AUTHOR WITH STEPHEN KING FOR
NEW YORK TIMES BESTSELLING GWENDY'S BUTTON BOX

"Tim Chizmar is a creative force of unbridled intensity. Every project he turns his hand to he makes his own. His writing is no exception and he is swiftly spiraling upward to dizzying horrific heights. A writer to keep an eye on with one caveat... Mr. Chizmar is not for the faint of heart. Consider yourself warned."

— P.S. GIFFORD, AUTHOR OF CURIOUSLY TWISTED
TALES: A SMATTERING OF P.S. GIFFORD

"There are authors of horror, who write creative, interesting stories, and then there is Tim Chizmar. Using his macabre imagination, Tim takes his readers to the darkest realms and makes them want to live there because his stories are so fascinating!"

— LIBBY GRANDY, AUTHOR OF DESERT SOLILOQUY,
PROMISES TO KEEP, AND LYDIA

"Tim Chizmar will lead you on a dark ride through nightmares, hellish landscapes, demon-infested planes, and the dark recesses of the mind. He'll leave you scared and smiling, running back to the line to buy another ticket."

— MICHAEL PAUL GONZALEZ, AUTHOR OF ANGEL FALLS
AND MISS MASSACRE'S GUIDE TO MURDER AND
VENGEANCE

"The danger of reading horror fiction is that you never know what's lurking on that next page. Like the protagonists in the stories themselves, any moment you could find your boundaries stretched, cracked, or ripped asunder. And so I have to advise you not to read the work of Tim Chizmar because I can guarantee that it will melt your face off with sheer awesomeness. If you're okay with being faceless, then please read on. In my opinion, it's a good trade off."

— BRAD C. HODSON, AUTHOR OF DARLING AND THE
MUD ANGEL

"At Troma we pride ourselves on recognizing the future Hollywood talents of tomorrow, Tim Chizmar is one of these, with his wild ideas and never ending insanity he will be a force to be reckoned with on the scare scene for years to come. He scares me."

— LLOYD KAUFMAN, PRESIDENT OF TROMA ENTERTAINMENT AND CREATOR OF THE TOXIC AVENGER

"When it comes to demons, vampires and other things that go bump in the night (especially things that you may not yet know and bumps you may have not yet heard), Chizmar is a young master honing his craft on the brittle edges of your various fears.

— BARNEY COHEN, SCREENWRITER OF "FRIDAY THE 13: THE FINAL CHAPTER" AND THE CREATOR OF "FOREVER KNIGHT"

"Tim Chizmar is batshit crazy and brilliant in the same breath. Long may he rage!"

— CHARLES BAND, PRESIDENT OF FULL MOON ENTERTAINMENT, CREATOR OF THE PUPPET MASTER SERIES

"Tim Chizmar's writing bristles with a barely harnessed energy, threatening to break free and run wild at any moment. It feels dangerous, like driving fast down the freeway against traffic. It seems like it could go wrong at any moment, but the story arrives intact to a satisfying and often surprising conclusion."

— IAN WELKE, AUTHOR OF THE WHISPERER IN DISSONANCE AND END TIMES AT RIDGEMONT HIGH

"Chizmar's talent is for writing characters who demand your attention, pulling you into their stories and the horrific journeys they go through. His ability to write realistic dialogue in an extraordinarily haunting way sets him far apart from a lot of today's writers. Hands down, one of the most entertaining and colorful up and coming authors in the genre, Tim is someone to watch, as it's apparent that he'll be around for a long, LONG time."

— JERRY SMITH, EDITOR IN CHIEF AT ICONS OF FRIGHT, FREELANCE WRITER/FANGORIA, DELIRIUM MAGAZINE, SCREENWRITER FOR VARMINT

"Tim Chizmar is a whirlwind of imagination, energy, and madness—and the stories he writes are every bit as imaginative, energetic, and mad as the man himself."

— MARTIN LASTRAPES, AUTHOR OF THE VAMPIRE AND THE HUNTER TRILOGY AND INSIDE THE OUTSIDE

"Tim Chizmar proves an impressive talent in genre fiction, an emerging voice that is heard as equal parts wit, insight, and artistry."

— Eric J. Guinard, Bram Stoker Award-winner
and a finalist for the International Thriller
Writers Award

"Tim writes with diabolical gusto and a flair for the macabre."

— Nigel McGuinness, former Ring of Honor
Champion and WWE commentator

"Chizmar's stories show great imagination and break creative boundaries, while still staying grounded in the human condition."

— Eric Miller, Editor "Hell Comes to Hollywood
1 & 2"

"You're called into the tent by an irresistible pitch. You sit down, the best seats in the house. When the lights dim, what you see might crawl under the membrane of your brain and root inside. But you won't be able to forget Tim's stories. And for those who love examining what's inside the dark, that's a good thing."

— John Palisano, Vice President of the Horror
Writers Association, Author of Dust of the Dead
and Ghost Heart

"I have spent most of my life engaging with real people on their true and terrifying testimonials of paranormal abuse and terror, yet Tim Chizmar has swam deep into the cold and dark abyss and dragged back something so traumatic and brutal that it makes my skin crawl. Tim Chizmar is a man who has slapped decency in the face… He is a man that has truly mastered the art of horror."

— G.L. DAVIES, AUTHOR OF GHOST SEX: THE VIOLATION

"I still have visions of Tim Chizmar's work and creations. They have driven all the freaks out of my life."

— JOEL M. REED, WRITER/DIRECTOR OF THE CULT CLASSIC BLOODSUCKING FREAKS

"Tim Chizmar's work speaks for itself… in a high-pitched Banshee wail that chills the soul, rattles your teeth and flays the living flesh from your quivering bones. And he somehow managed this with wry, twisted humor that makes you laugh nervously as you piss your pants in fright! Great stuff!"

— JERYD POJAWA, TWO TIME ACADEMY AWARD WINNING ART DIRECTOR, THE ABYSS AND TERMINATOR 2

"Tim Chizmar brings traditional horror into the 21st century with the casual effortlessness literary voice of a modern blogger and an eye for terror that touches on our most ancient, cave-dark fears."

— DYLAN BRODY, HUMORIST AND AUTHOR OF LASTS LAST

"Tim Chizmar is on my bucket list. I want to kill him with a bucket... the one I vomited into violently after reading stories so terrifying that I literally pulled out my eyes and stuck them in my ass, so I could watch as I shit myself. Chizmar's writing weill cause permamintt brian dalmedgee"

— ROBERT CORPSY RHINE, DEADITOR-IN-CHIEF OF GIRLS AND CORPSES MAGAZINE

"Tim is the quintessential evil clown. A natural story weaver, a yarn spinner- but beware his faux-friendly demeanor! Don't get drawn in when he flashes that smile. Look closer and see the dark, twisted glint in his eye for it is here that he will capture your soul. If you choose to follow him down the rabbit hole into his sick, maddening world, you must do so gladly for you may never return. If you love horrible things you will love Tim Chizmar!!"

— KATARINA LEIGH WATERS, WWE DIVA, AND STORY CONTRIBUTOR TO HELL COMES TO HOLLYWOOD 2

"Tim Chizmar, as witnesses will agree, is nearly as terrifying as his writings; nearly."

— FANGORIA MAGAZINE

"Tim Chizmar is a Master Thought Criminal. The devastating impact he inflicts on the reader can be summed up in just one word: Mind-rape."

— LARRY WESSEL, PRIEST OF CHURCH OF SATAN

"Tim Chizmar has found the perfect outlet for his wicked sense of humor—the pages of fantasy fiction. Demons, devils and humans join Tim's circus with echoes of Faust and Dante. Buy a ticket."

— Steve Mazan, Emmy-winning comedy writer, & author of Dying To Do Letterman

"Is it weird that I fantasize about breaking Tim Chizmar's neck? …Especially after I read his crap. P.S. put some clothes on you're scaring the children!"

— Sinn Bodhi, WWE Superstar, the Warlord of Weird and creator of Las Vegas' Freakshow Wrestling

"Tim Chizmar is an amazing author. He pulls his readers inch-by-inch into an increasingly deepening and darkening precarious place - and then shocks them with a level of fear far beyond their expectations. I refer to his books as a 'heart attack in a book.'"

— Rock Riddle, Amazon #1 Best-Selling Author How to Become a Magnet to Hollywood Success.

"Tim Chizmar is the face of horror comics. He has a raw and biting wit that will make the hairs on the back of your neck stand up in fear. Tim is unafraid to make readers face the naked truth and shock them with story twists that will keep them guessing."

— Rik Offenberger, Editor-in-Chief First Comics News

"How about Tim Chizmar – isn't he a great host? I want to thank Tim, I have not seen this many people in the club; I do a show every Wednesday I'm lucky to fill up a booth!"

— Jon Lovitz, Saturday Night Live Alum, Star of
The Critic

"You gotta hand it to the guy. He believed it. He achieved it. You can't hold the guy back. Tim and I have several things in common. We both are among the few who go for it. We both saw a much bigger picture for ourselves than what our peers saw. We dreamed and we followed. That's what people like us do and without dream followers, the standard of what can be accomplished is compromised. We know better. Because this common ground is so mission driven, I will always be in support of Tim and his many adventures. I hope this book is his biggest success yet! As he continues to add title after title to his accomplishments and career, I want him to now that I have his back . . ."

— Rob VanDam, Former ECW & World
Wrestling Entertainment Champion

"I first met Tim Chizmar when I was pretty fresh to the LA comedy scene, and he welcomed me with open arms. Tim is like the perfect horror movie--He's such a jolly, heartwarming guy who will always put a smile on your face... you'll have no idea how disturbed and twisted he can be. THEN, he springs it on you, and you love it!"

— Natalie Palamides, Comedian and voice of
Buttercup, The PowerPuff Girls

"Mr. Chizmar is charismatic and a down right funny guy. I had the pleasure of sharing a hotel room with him once. Kept me in stitches but don't let him take his shoes off."

— ALEXANDRA KUBE, EMMY-WINNING ARTIST PINKY AND THE BRAIN

"Tim Chizmar…I would hate for you to be the guy behind me in bumper to bumper traffic, I have a feeling I'd be up against the guard rail."

— JEFF FOXWORTHY, COMEDIAN AND STAR OF THE BLUE COLLAR COMEDY TOUR

"I would especially never read anything by Tim, that's bottom of the barrel, I don't go in that direction."

— KEVIN SMITH, WRITER/DIRECTOR OF CLERKS, TUSK, ETC

"Tim Chizmar is crazy with imagination and has an awesome way with words. If you don't give his book a chance I got two words for you, Super Kick!! If you're not down with that I got two more words for you, Suck It!"

— NICK JACKSON, IWGP AND RING OF HONOR TAG CHAMPION, THE YOUNG BUCKS

SPOOKYNINJAKITTY BOOKS BY

TIM CHIZMAR

Modern Madness:

Gateway to the Grotesque

Modern Madness 2:

The Screaming Virgins

California Dreaming:

A Personal Inquiry into Happiness –OR– How a miserable self-absorbed egomaniac killed his "Me Monster" in the Idaho Mountains

Marissa Cross Book 1:

A NecRomantic Novel

Marissa Cross Book 2:

A NecRomantic Sequel

PERFECT is the ENEMY of DONE:

How to get out of your own damn way and write the book

SOUL TRAITOR

TIM CHIZMAR

*Dedicated to Sinn Bodhi & Karen Kreep
Your kindness and belief in my art
means more than you'll ever know.
You are good people... sorry about your microwave.*

*Also for J.G. Moore, thanks for reminding me to write this fucker,
Now it's your turn. PS- I'm straight...*

CONTENTS

"Our father who art in heaven
Stay there
And we will stay on Earth
Which is sometimes so pretty"

— Jacques Prevert

ONE

Jessica Ro sat naked on her lawn chair with her laptop sitting on the little plastic table out in front of her. Her knees pushed together, toes curled, awkwardly digging into the grass as if to propel her ideas to the surface. The cheap plastic table was pink just like everything else at the cabin she'd rented for the month. Pink toaster, pink doilies, pink plastic flowers, pink, pink, pink; even the key and keychain she been given was the girlie color. The cabin itself was also painted pink. Each of the cabins at the family nudist resort had been painted a different color to readily identify it to staff and visitors. Staff at *The Garden of Eden* called the cabins birdhouses, based on their angular shape and pointy roof. This was one of the reasons Jessica had chosen it. She came here to write what would no doubt be her greatest novel ever, or so she hoped. She stared at the blank Word doc and then lost herself in the worlds of fantasy and make-believe as she began to type. Real life sucked for her, so writing had always been an escape. With all of her raw red-headed beauty she was still shy, quiet and defiantly weird. She had absolutely no instinct for seduction, and in the last few years even called herself asexual to ward off suitors. Its not that Jessica didn't enjoy intimacy; its just that she could never savor the moment enough to let go. She was always over thinking what everything meant. Ask Derek Fuckface, her ex. Fuckface was her adorable new nickname for him ever since he lied, cheated, and screwed her over. As she second guessed her life, it spilled over into the words she typed onto the glowing screen. This all was her plague. Was she afraid of success? Was she just a shitty writer? A shitty person who happened to be a writer?

The Mount Baldy Mountains rose and fell around her in majestic mostly green splendor as the sun began to set on her pink table. Most of her day had been spent getting there from the hustle and bustle of Los Angeles. It was never a fun commute but listening to a little Celine Dion helped to lessen the blow. Her Jeep had guzzled too much gas on the way. The incessant, angry insect buzz of her oversized tires interfered with Celine's voice. The sound was cool though; like the little Jeep was humming a mantra to the sizzling blacktop. She cranked the volume up all the while thinking to herself, *its better than sitting in L.A traffic*. Celine's voice reminded her of Las Vegas and The Venetian. Powerful memories of luck and alcohol induced fun; Hunter S. Thompson had it right. What a town. She had recalled the casino where she'd seen Celine's show, and where Jessica Ro had expected to wind up in the sack with some meathead rebound self-serving man-child that was barely able to read anything more than a Muscle & Fitness magazine. The Vegas adventure that was supposed to help wash Derek er ah... *Fuckface*'s memory away and give her some raunchy life experiences to write about, two birds, one stone. She saw Celine but found no handsome mindless hunks to spirit her off to wild nights of unbridled passion. No birds. Not even a god damned stone. Screw it. Jessica could find the most peculiar details to cling to, to help coat a lame memory with a hint of amusement. Jessica got up from the pink setting and walked to the hill's edge overlooking the community of naked folks milling about. She enjoyed being in the buff with her skin exposed. It was funny to think that textiles as the other nudists called them, would call her a naked woman right now, yet we don't cry when there's a naked dog or a naked horse! Clothing was the unnatural part. Hell, if god had wanted us naked we would have been born that way. Jessica laughed to herself as she noticed her engaged friends David and Chrissy. They waved at each other as Jessica's mind wandered back to Vegas.

The Celine billboard off of the I-15 heading into Sin City had a picture of Celine's back, just her back. Not her face over the shoulder looking all Celine-ish and French and singery. The ad was just a photo of Celine's back. The caption read, wait for it, 'Celine's back!' Ridiculous, Jessica had thought, *Idiots! Even I could think of something better than that!* This silly memory gave her hope that her soon to be written novel would astound readers worldwide. She hoped. Her life had to add up to something worthwhile otherwise it had all been a colossal cosmic joke. This is why she liked to escape for the perfect writing setting, strip off all the literal and figurative baggage and let loose at *The Garden of Eden*. The drive up the mountain in the jeep had all been worth it to drive up to the gate of her favorite nudist resort and quickly check-in. It was earthy, rustic; kind of like the resort from the old film Dirty Dancing. In ways Jessica Ro felt very much like the character Baby; quirky and unaware of how badly she needed to unhinge. Nobody puts Baby in a corner, yeah right, hell; Jessica always puts Jessica in a corner. She'd chosen to come on a Monday to the getaway as most of the weekend vacation folks would be gone and it'd be only the few hundred spirited souls that live on the grounds on the grid in mobile homes and campers. Probably fugitives and outlaws she imagined hiding from the crimes of passion. Not likely in the real world as they were called 'dirty hippies' or 'perverts' from upstanding community members but to her they were free spirits and after years of visiting, some were practically family, like David and Chrissy who were engaged to be married very soon. They were organizing a big event at Black's Beach in San Diego.

Black's was a nudist oasis of sports, cookouts, surfing, suntans and fun. All 'au naturel the way life should be. This was a way of life for these people. Most found it more freeing than sexy.

Her long red hair was caught up in a gust of wind and she closed her eyes thoroughly enjoying it. Her red-gold locks tickled her as it swirled over her. She exhaled all the troubles in the world, letting the negativity leave her. The breakup with *Fuckface*, the three book deal she had lost, and the truth of needing to borrow money from her friends to pay her over-flowing bills. Owing her friends money was not exactly part of the glamorous Hollywood lifestyle she had envisioned when she left Pennsylvania ten years ago. There were no giant billboards throughout Hollywood showcasing the subtle freckles that decorated her perfect cheekbones. No poster of her holding her latest best-selling novel for college kids to masturbate to. Fifty Shades of… nope. No paparazzi snapping shots of her walking the red carpet for her latest best-selling novel adapted into a crappy high budget flick. She was not sought after in the least. Nobody was thinking of her for anything. Her Facebook friends still considered her a big success because she'd sold a few short stories and a handful of articles, plus there was that one game show she was on a few years back. Friends loved pulling it up from YouTube at parties to play along with her. She always wanted to be a success with her career and relationships and when both didn't come in over a decade of trying she felt like a fraud, in both the writing industry and in the bedroom, but that's why she was here now at this birdhouse in these mountains. No more talking about it, *Fuckface* was long gone it was time to do the other, she knew she had a good bestseller in her bones and goddammit it was time to show everyone she could do it. Screw Derek times infinity.

Petite, freckled, redheaded Jessica Ro closed the laptop and went in to her pink birdhouse. It was cool and dark now. She unzipped her bag and took out a pink t-shirt that flattered her very slight curves and purple sandals. She tossed the pink aside and took out another shirt, *dear god anything but more pink*. She settled on tie-dye and caught a glimpse of herself in the long mirror. Being bottomless gave her a breezy feel of freedom. The tuff of natural hair was nice too; validating that red was her natural hair color. She wished she could shun all norms and grow armpit hair too, but she wasn't ready for the criticism. Grabbing her weathered and worn old brown towel (essential at any nudist resort if you ever plan to sit) she began the short hike towards the kitchen/restaurant area.

Although typically not open aside from weekends, the owner had agreed to make an exception for her so the two could meet up for a bite at least occasionally during her stay. The trees sang seductively to her as she made it from the grassy hilltop to the trail. She passed a few people of varying ages, races, and body types before she made it to the door of the dining area. Mr. Jenkins stood reading a newspaper at the door. He had a big nose and a little penis. He was proud like a peacock. The stubble of his skinny face looked sharp enough to rub the paint off of a car. He smiled at Jessica and she smiled back. She kept her giggles on the inside as not to offend. On the weekends there were specials designed to keep down the separate food orders but today wasn't one of those, so she wasn't sure what she would have tonight. She tried being a vegan. But let's face it, when you've grown up on Big Macs, can you ever truly put that demon down.

Inside the dining area she saw one of the younger girls from the resort now working the kitchen area. Jessica put in her order and went to the outside area by the pool. The thoughts of failure trailed off into the obscure recesses of her mind while she looked at the pool. The shell designed tiles hiding at the bottom of the pool and the handful of naked swimmers swayed oddly to the tunes playing in the background. More and more bodies left the pool as it got darker and hopped to the hot tub area. The Stantons and another middle-eastern looking couple whose names she didn't know turned fat then skinny then fat again in the ripples of the distorting water. *A liquid funhouse mirror,* she thought. At the far end our dreamer saw the owner of the resort, Evelyn, waving in her direction as she got out of the pool.

"Hey, honey, I missed you," Evelyn exclaimed as she rushed her way, giving her a great big wet naked hug. Evelyn was a plump older lady who appeared to be in her later fifties, although nobody would dare ask exactly how old she was, that's impolite. Evelyn was a lifelong nudist who had inherited *The Garden of Eden* from her father as the story went. Her white skin was smooth porcelain and nearly flawless aside from a few weathered age spots. Evelyn's breasts hung slightly lower than had in years past, and on her stomach, there were signs of childbirth; kitty cat scratches as she referred to them. Her hair was dyed blonde and in braids. As *over the hill* as she might seem at first glance, her green eyes told a different story. She had an at-oneness with everything that Jessica admired.

"I missed you too" the redhead said, putting her towel down and then taking a seat at a pink lawn chair near the pool. Then with a jolt of annoyance she switched to a neon green chair to keep from this semblance of order, "Hey, aren't you cold?"

"Sun hasn't set yet on this old bird," Evelyn exclaimed while diving back into the water. The pool seemed to catch her with open arms. She belonged there. Jessica wished she belonged somewhere. *The Garden of Eden* was as good as any place for right now. Beggars can't be choosers.

It was just the two of them now at the swimming pool although farther away she saw that the gathering near the hot tub area had grown into quite a party spot. She could smell a familiar scent of marijuana wafting in the air. Jessica watched as a couple of families had their kids packing up to leave after a long day of fun in the sun. She wished she'd known this kind of freedom as a child, wished she'd grown up without the societal shackles of fear and a loathing for her own body. Even though Jessica had the slender body many dreamed of her shame had kept her a prisoner in her own mind for years. Nowadays she had accepted herself; he was petite with modest B cup breasts adorned with pokey tiny nipples. She had long legs, but not particularly tall. As she sat by the pool waiting on her meal order her knees again pushed together concealing that patch of red hair. She intentionally opened her legs embracing the reminder that dammit nude isn't lewd, and she could sit how she wanted, especially here of all places. It was funny how one chance encounter with a nude art model had opened her eyes. Jacques. He smelled like cigarettes but was much prettier than he was handsome. She caught herself and recognized that she should be thinking about her damn book that wasn't here yet. *Fuck you Derek.*

"Lost in thought there, Red?" The old lady came up from the pool, dripping water off her body.

"Yeah, look at that family," Jessica gestured at the family storing the bad mitten net away. "No shame, no secrets, just honest body acceptance."

"…and love, that's how it should be. That's how we like it here. You know that Andrews family are third generation nudists."

"Wow, really? I wouldn't mind having that, plus a bestseller."

"Yes, you and your writing," She chuckled. "As for them, I had the pleasure of welcoming their grandpa and grandma here a long time ago."

"That's so cool." She dipped her foot into the inviting pool water thinking *How freakin old is Evelyn*? She carried it well nonetheless.

"So how is the book coming, you getting work done in the pink cabin?"

"Ha, the pink world, yeah I think so. I just got here, but, yeah, I know what I want to do with it."

"The astronauts book, right; vampires?" Water glistened off of the voluptuous older lady. She was most likely a real heartbreaker once. Jessica savored this observation. It was apparent. Her overall natural confidence had sex appeal. Evelyn would make a great character in her book.

"Kinda, it's more like reverse vampires. You see these [she loved the opportunity to go on about the idea, always easier than writing it down] astronauts go up in space . . ." She was enjoying opening up to her friend. She could tell the older lady truly enjoyed hearing her ideas and wasn't just humoring her as other did.

"There's a dog in it too, right?"

"Hosehead, yes, good memory! He's important – that's Hosehead."

"What an odd name for a dog," Evelyn commented, shaking her wet hair like a big ol' canine herself.

"He's named after my friend Rhett's dog." This made her smile. In real life, Hosehead was a white big Siberian husky with urinary problems but had always been a huge Jessica Ro fan. The real Hosehead was also a male. She wanted to keep Hosehead's real name in the story as a testament to her friend and the dog that adored her. "Anyway, it's the four astronauts and Hoser."

"I thought you said he was Hosehead?" Evelyn's smile was genuine but playful.

"That's his nickname," Jessica hollered. She had put a lot of thought into Hoser. He would be her Lassie; metaphorically and literally.

"Look, so anyway, there's the five of them and they go off into space, but there's this black hole they hadn't counted on and it sucks them in." Evelyn gave her full attention as she prattled on. She may or may not have understood what was coming out of Jessica's mouth, but she definitely enjoyed the way it opened up her soul to be seen more clearly. "… and so, they come out and think nothing is wrong and they head back to earth…"

She stopped for a beat to accentuate her next bit of fictional cleverness. "Except instead of a blue-ish earth the planet looks red-ish." Then another dramatic pause from the quirky excitable red head.

Evelyn's penciled in eyebrows raised as if to clear her into proceeding. "They crash land and discover that all of the oceans are full of blood. Blood! These humans, the astronauts discover, have water in their bodies that flush the blood they drink around in their systems! So, these astronauts try to fit in but in order to survive now they have to secure water from bodies or at blood banks! She was so excited with her story knowing for sure it was the greatest thing ever. The masses will eat this up.

"I see, and I remember there's something in that with the big dog too, right?" Evelyn enjoyed the way Jessica's eyes gleefully flared every time the name Hosehead was mentioned. The redhead pulled her knees up to her chest and she squeezed them close as she blurted out more.

"Yes! Every time there's a full moon he changes into a man. A man! See 'cause he's a reverse werewolf, too, just like the vampires." She was using jazz hands to bring home her narrative to the lady.

"Genius," Evelyn said clapping. "You'll be a millionaire."

"God, I hope so or at least be able to pay my bills" She got serious. "I need this to work out, I'm at my breaking point in LA I can't keep struggling like I am. It's so hard." Evelyn knew that tears were immanent. She didn't want to open the flood gates, but she couldn't hold it back, Jessica started crying. The wise old nudist lady leaned over from where she was next to the pool to comfort the fragile red headed writer.

"There, there, kiddo," she held her and rocked back and forth. Evelyn had a wise and soothing aura about her. She never spoke of children but would have probably made the greatest mom ever.

The food service girl from the kitchen interrupted with Jessica's food order. "Here's your food, ma'am."

"Thank you, Katie. Please just put it over there." Evelyn motioned to her. The woman placed the tray on a nearby countertop. The girl scurried away trying to ignore the drama of another crying naked patron.

"I'm sorry for breaking down like this, I'm so embarrassed, but with Derek and I, I can't, I just…" She began to cry again, that uncontrollable sort of cry that makes it so you can't even talk. Her voice squeaked as she tried to get words out.

"Shhh, let it out. He's a fool to lose you like that. It was over some bullshit low budget horror movie, right?"

Jessica began to compose herself, "He's a fuckface, and he lied to me. They all lie, fucking men."

"Oh honey," Evelyn rubbed this young girl's back. 'You're far too young and talented and beautiful to even think like that. Well, besides my place is a stress-free zone, and look at this good food. That grub over there smells delicious."

The tray had just what she'd ordered, a grilled ham and cheese sandwich on sourdough cut in half with some mystery sauce in a cup to dip it in, potato salad with paprika sprinkled on top, plus three delicious pickle slices on the side. She also had a cup of unsweetened ice tea, and for desert a cup of rainbow sherbet. If it all tasted as good as it looked she knew she'd be in heaven. For such a petite girl she often wondered where the food went because she could eat. She took a sip of her tea as Evelyn spoke of the trials and tribulations of running the resort to distract her.

"The committees and elections," Evelyn's hands flailed dramatically, "The various dramas within nudist organizations are absolutely laughable. You'd think we would be on the same page but instead everybody refuses to work together."

She continued with her fists on hips. "Of course, there are the recent repairs to the place. Earl, that little shyster is always trying to give excuses for why things aren't done around here. He's just so gosh darn slow. I wanna bust his stupid little balls, but I don't. That's not how this classy lady rolls. He'd probably cry and that's not what I want to be responsible for. I like to create solutions not more problems. My father instilled in me that any idiot can destroy but it takes a true kind and creative person to build. Destroying Earl is not on my to-do list. But darling, let me tell you, he moves slower then molasses up hill in winter; there's no getting thru to him or really most of the board for that matter. As Mr. Jones would put it, talking to some of those people is like . . ."

This banter was working on Jessica. She was starting to laugh and forget why she was crying in the first place. Evelyn was savvier then she let on. Her playful griping was a nothing more than misdirection to help Jessica regain her bearings. There was really nothing that Evelyn was really worried about, but Jessica Ro didn't need to know that. She nearly choked when hearing a particularly amusing story about a new nudist discovering why putting on pants before entering the cactus maze might be a good idea. Good old Jake Wilkinson and his thorny ass was enough to put anyone in a better mood. Towards the end of the hour the writer felt a lot better. Freckles began to reappear as her cheeks became less flushed. Before finally heading off, she had to inquire about the oddest guest staying at the resort, "How's Nakey these days?"

Evelyn's face lit up with the kind of excitement she had while describing her novel idea. Evelyn loved Nakey. They were life partners so to speak. She understood Nakey and Nakey understood her. He knew her deepest secrets and always offered solutions. "Oh, he's great, just as cool as ever. I'm sure you'll see me with him at some point. I'll bring him to visit you."

Evelyn loved her pet boa constrictor and was never as happy as when it would slide around her body. Nakey knew her like nobody else in the world. She loved showing him off and having kids discover that a snake is not slimy and gross but rather smooth to the touch. He was responsive like a dog and finicky like a cat, if there were such a thing as a twelve-foot long, scaly cat. Jessica thought having a snake as a pet was odd but who was she to judge. Whatever floats her boat, besides she'd dated a few *snakes* herself in the past. Nakey would never pull a Derek and lie. Animals, or in this case serpents would never do something like that. They are pure and simple. If only the human men in her life could be that way.

"I'd like that." Jessica lied. "Thanks for listening; I bet Nakey is a great listener too."

"He is most of the time. You know I'm always available for you anytime, yours is a very powerful soul and I'm encouraged just being in your presence; now you better go run off and get some writing done. Next time I see you, I want to hear who's gonna be playing Hosehead, in his man-form, on the big screen when they adapt your soon-to-be written award-winning novel."

The seminude, bare bottom redhead stood from the towel she'd been sitting on and began to gather the nearly empty food tray and trash. She smiled at the old lady as various handsome actors danced through her mind. "Leave it, I'll get it on the way back through." So, she did.

On her way back to the trail Jessica saw a little commotion at one of the cabins, some music and fun around a fireplace. The flames licked up into the air. The sun had completely set over the rustic getaway; it was now full on night. The night stars shine so much more brightly in the country when not washed out by the vast city street lights. The trees blanketed the sky. Crickets sang out to Jessica from all around her. The universe was watching. She suddenly felt small in a good way for a change. A few of the guests recognized her from past events and called to her but she waved but kept walking. When she got to the birdhouse in the land of epic pink, she lay on the bed dreaming of success and opportunity. When she had drifted off to sleep, it hadn't occurred to her that a single word hadn't been added to the story.

In the morning she gathered her things with a rejuvenated sense of self-worth and swore to attack Hollywood with more gusto than every before. She drove the gas guzzling jeep back through the freeways of overstuffed wannabes all the time knowing she was different, because she had talent. With Celine Dion's greatest hits cheering her on she got to her tiny one bedroom rented room in North Hollywood and bounded up the outside steps to the door. That's when she saw the note posted:

This is NELLY, why you not answer phone?
I call and call. It's been six months and no rent.
This cannot continue, call me by Friday night or you
NEED to find other place to stay.
I cannot continue this. No good for me.

"Shit," Jessica exclaimed. This day was now Monday and under a black garbage bag she could tell that her few possessions had been dumped on the yard. Still, she tried the doorknob anyway and as predicted her key no longer worked. She went back to the resort; she knew Evelyn would take pity on her plight, though it was of her own making.

Later, Jessica was fully nude again caught up in conversation at the main clubhouse.

"And then the astronaut . . ."

Jessica inhaled a big gulp of air to refuel her words, but before she could go on Heath chimed in, "Wait, what were the astronauts names again?"

"Reed, Sue, Ben, and Johnny. Why?"

He laughed and a few others around the table joined him, "MARVELous names. You know that's copyrighted?" Zach was scratching his beard not wanting to burst her bubble.

"What?" Her knees somehow knew to push together. They almost had a mind of their own.

"Are you serious? Reed, Sue, Ben, and Johnny?! That's *The Fantastic Four*!"

"The Fantastic… what?"

"Four- as in you might get sued four times," he laughed. "You can't steal their idea."

"Do they have a dog?"

"No, no dogs but they have a giant-ass legal team. MARVEL would seriously kick your ass. Change the names," he said while guzzling a beer.

Jessica shook her head in disbelief and with a sad pouty face said, "They don't have reverse vampires do they?" She leaned into Zach to hide under his arm.

"Nope, that great idea is all yours." He turned from her before staring at her breasts and saying, "By the way those are really working for me."

She was less than impressed with the *charm* but smiled anyway, after the copyright snafu, she decided it was time to stumble home and didn't want to be alone just yet.

"I'll walk you. We can think of astronaut names along the way," Zach piped up while gently pulling her to her feet from the blue bench they were curled up together on. Heath burped again as his way of acknowledging Zach. Kat threw a handful of potato chips at Heath which said it all. The security guard started walking their way again.

"You fuckers are gonna get kicked out," Zach said as he left with his newly won-over redheaded prize on his arm. A few minutes passed. Jessica was still a bit upset but was starting to relax as she and Zach walked a ways into the sea of colorful personalities.

"Don't let that douche get under your skin girl. If you let anyone bug you like that then they win."

"Yeah right."

"Look, your ideas are really cool," he chuckled, "But you wa . . ."

"No, it sucks! You're still laughing too," interrupted Jessica pulling away from him haphazardly. Zach didn't let go of her arm in a playful yet detaining way.

"I'm not laughing at you I'm laughing at me. You wanna know why? Your idea is really cool. I'm not lying. I have a weird hobby. You just kinda made me realize it is silly and maybe it sucks. Reverse Vampires are awesome. It's a great idea. My hobby not so awesome, you wanna hear?"

"Let's have it, boy."

"Okay, well I'm a hands-on guy but I love art. As you know, I work as a lightening grip. I'm good with my hands, but artistic? Mmm not so much. My cousin is a shoe repair guy. He showed me back in the day how to fix my work boots that I was always fucking up on set. Those things, good ones can be expensive."

"Okay . . ."

"Yeah, I would re-sole them and add leather cuffs, so they wouldn't dig into the back of my legs. And I . . ."

"Why is this sucky? This sounds useful, pretty clever."

"Well, here's where it gets odd. I started thinking what else I could attach to the boots. The old ones I didn't wear anymore. Just to be silly, stupid shit. You know? Boot art. I make art from boots." She didn't laugh at all.

"What kind of stuff would you stick to them?" she asked. She wasn't sure if she was curious or confirming that his boot art was in fact suckier then her book idea.

"I would glue on mouse traps, candle holders, those little bobbly Hawaiian girls that you stick to your dash board. Whatever I can find that pops out at me in thrift stores. I use this shoe glue that is brutal I got from my cousin. It works on everything. If you're not careful with it will rip the skin right off of your hands." She smiled, "Okay, tell me I'm right Jess. My boot art idea is totally retarded right? I told you."

She looked at Zach with her best version of bedroom eyes, "So, you're good with your hands?"

"Ha. I have some that I'm working on back at my birdhouse if you wanna see?"

She pulled him close as she continued down the road in the direction of his brief oasis on the way.

Entering the room, the couple couldn't keep their hands off of each other. He kissed her backing her up to the pink kitchen table. Her hands gripped the edge of the weak pink chairs tucked under it. His cabin was closer to hers they both realized and also adorned in pink furniture. They were giggling and panting. Things were starting to go from playful to steamy. He turned her around, started kissing her neck. Her body was ready for this. She needed what was yet to come.

"If you care, there is my awesomely crappy boot art." He never thought that sentence would come out in the form of sweet nothings.

Her eyes practically rolled into the back of her head, "It's awesome."

The problem was that there was really nothing 'slick' about her. She picked up a boot with a bunch of tiny umbrellas stuck to it and examined it curiously.

"You're right. This stuff sticks to everything. Would this stuff work on my leather book bag? I freakin' ripped it the other day. It's my favorite; had it since freshmen year. It's in my cabin."

"Yup," Zach picking up a one-gallon canister of shoe epoxy. "Come on. I'll do it for now. You don't want this shit on you at all. It's a bitch to handle, you need gloves."

"Lovely."

A few minutes later Jessica and Zach are in her pink cabin sitting on pink chairs repairing her favorite book bag. Jessica searched for something interesting to say but was unsuccessful. Zach swiftly worked his magic and the book bag was as good as new.

"Viola!" Zach blurted.

"It was a gift from my favorite English Lit professor. However can I thank you?"

"You can thank me the exact same way you thanked your professor."

"Come again?"

"Well, seeing as how you retardedly reinvented the Fantastic Four I can only imagine you didn't get A's by handing in original work. I'm guessing your oral skills were your strong suit."

"You, asshole."

"JK! Just teasing you Jessica. Jeez. Take a joke. Relax. Ask yourself, what would Reid, Sue, Johnny and Ben do? He then let out a creepy laugh that made her very uncomfortable.

"I think you need to get out. Get some sleep you gotta get up early tomorrow. You know I was going to sleep with until you turned into an asstard! Do all guys turn into freakin' idiots after midnight? Jessica shoved Zach towards the door. Suddenly, Zach hands latched onto her arms like two string snakes. She was defenseless in his grip.

"What the fuck do you think you're doing? Get the fuck outta here before I scream, you, dickhead!"

"I like that fire. Where has that been all evening?"

"Fuck you!"

"After you suck my dick. Book bag. I know what girls like you are like." He was hard now. She could feel his cock pressing against her leg.

Her fists were futile. He was strong. She realized quickly that this situation was real. Do something. Anything. She reached behind her, her fingers searching for something to grab to use as a weapon. Boot art. She knew exactly what she had in her petite hand, irony! She swung the boot at his jaw. His grip released. He was disoriented. The front porch was right there. If only she could get him outside for a split second, then she could lock the door and wash away this awful situation. She shoved him hard to make some space between them. In an instant he was frozen against the wall to the left of the door. Why wasn't he moving? He straightened as if his tendons were suddenly too short for his limbs. What was he doing, she thought? His eyes were wide and ferocious. But he was still. Still. His fingers were twisted, almost claw-like. What the fuck? She should run. Should not wait to see what he was up to, but for some inexplicable reason she didn't.

"Zach?"

The side of Zach's head was fixed against the wall as if he was listening for mice crawling on the pipes inside. Except he wasn't…

Jessica upon further inspection realized that his temple had been impaled by one of the coat rack hooks next to the door.

Zach was dead. Out of nowhere, Zach was dead.

"Holy shit. Holy shit, holy shit holy shit, shit, shit, shit, holy shit!"

In the movies you might scream for joy at a discovery like this but in real life things play out so much differently than you would expect. Jessica was stupefied. She was in disbelief. She just murdered someone. She was overwhelmed. The same thing goes for what an actual dead body looks like. It looks fake. Rubbery. Dead bodies look so gruesome in the movies and on television. So much detail. But not in real life. Cheap wax dummies at best. He had been a person, but now the body.

Minutes flew by. She just stood there, staring, thinking while her instincts are all going haywire. The pink cabin taunted her with unanswerable silence. Jessica stood almost as still as the dead body in front of her. Finally, she opened a closet door not expecting to find any answers at all. Holding the closet door open she stared at her naked body in the mirror, with the red painted handprints on her breasts partially dripping down like blood. She thought of all the shit in her life: Derek and the breakup, avoiding her friend's calls from the ones she can't payback, being kicked out of her home and finally losing her book deal that she'd had for one full year. One full year of not being able to come through on her end to deliver the manuscripts. What the fuck was her problem. Maybe it was a stupid idea. Maybe it was just a rip-off. Where had she heard those names before? She'd come up here to get away and now she was more dragged down than ever before. On top of everything that was awful or pathetic in her life, she just fucking killed a man. Worst day ever!

"Fuck!" she screamed before crumpling into a ball on the wooden floor. Nobody loved her. Nobody understood her passion for something more than this life. If there's nothing left for her she figured she might as well be dead. She jumped to her feet. Should she keep moving? Should she stay still? The simplest of questions were unanswerable. Her brain was on overload.

Jessica fled into the kitchen. She took a knife out of the pink knife holder next to the pink toaster and stared at her wrists. Was she going to slit arms long ways, not in that pussy attention-getting way but in a serious, "I'm done here' way. No? No! Noooooo!!! No?"

Visions of her veins spilling like spaghetti all over the pink cutlery. She dropped the knife to the floor. Shaking. Too much fucked up shit for one person to take. Overload.

"I would give anything to have one bestselling book," She said aloud. "I would give anything to just be a success instead of a fail-ure." She looked around analyzing everything in sight. Her eyes caught the shoe epoxy and what lay behind it. Without hesitation she picked up the cleaning supplies bottle with the little Robones on it. She downed in quickly and lay choking to death on the floor naked and alone.

TWO

Hell can be a very uncomfortable place even for those at the top of the demonic food chain. Humans might have invented red tape, but Hell perfected it. If that isn't bad enough just imagine the celestial horseshit that comes with a place responsible for creating religion and politics? What genius devil or angel of war could conjure up religion; a thing that has claimed more lives than every disease combined thorough history?

Now try to wrap your mind around what a deceitful art the game of politics is and moreover who or what ravenous cosmic primadonna's brainchild such a thing could have been. Imagine what those monster's minds must be like? Take Damien-ki Zakire Monteloflobe for instance, a mild mannered but highly talented salesman, er, sales-demon, a very talented yet lackadaisical crea-ture. He simply went thru the motions and still had the wits to mind fuck more humans out of their souls than any other demon before him. Sales were in Damien-ki's veins or whatever things he had crawling inside of him in lieu of veins. He could sell ice to an Eskimo. He had human greed down to a science. He knew the ins and outs of greed's ins and outs. He knew his product and the demand for it. Every day in Hell was Black Friday when his sales report figures came in. His quotas for hitting the high marks of the prestigious 24 Club or 40 Club was child's play. On a good day an average demon might pull in X amount of souls—Whoopdie fuckin doo! Damien-ki Zakire Monteloflobe was known as the President of the 666 Club. His numbers were that damn good! Even that term did not do him justice, it just sounded cool, but his actual record was well over that and then some. Think about it. If Santa could deliver toys all over the world in a single night, what could a talented demonic salesman do? His success fed the office moral and water cooler gossip alike. The day he closed on a certain black United States President was a pretty big deal. His co-workers had brought him a cake for that one.

To say that Hell's sales staff was the best in the world is an understatement. Best in Infinity is much more accurate. Sales has always been the life blood of Hell, not just for Damien-ki Zakire Monteloflobe. The place flourished and that is putting it lightly. Why wouldn't it? Demons were encouraged to be proud. It was a sin after all, one of seven sweet ass inventions created by their Dark Lord: Pride. Some demons would do an End Zone victory dance; some would make it rain on a wedding day or put a fly in your Chardonnay as the song goes. One demon even wore a necklace of his victim's ears (clients) because he saw it in an action movie.

Most humans were asking for it anyway as far as Hell's employees were concerned. To them, there was nothing more beautiful and/or creatively violent as the human spirit. Importing souls was a commodity. "It's a buyer's market!" the sales staff would joke. Souls were sought after relentlessly, not that you need to sell Hell very much these days, mind you. Death and taxes are a given, however, after you croak the universe gives you a choice; pick door number one or door number two. Do you go up? Do you go down? On paper that sounds like an easy choice but not when sin has twisted you all up and your mind is a hornet's nest swarming with ego and confusion, unaccountability and regret. As often as a soul was ripe for the picking, every so often you get that person who is on the fence.

David Dow was one of those. It seemed obvious that he was heading south on his journey into the void however he was suddenly bitten by his conscience out of the blue. Dave had fucked everyone he knew in some way shape or form. People were practically ecstatic that he'd been stabbed by a faceless mugger. Dave had a day or so of introspection to think on his deathbed at Tampa General Hospital. Outside, nothing had changed. Palm trees still swayed in the tropical afternoon wind. Sand still got everywhere. He was still an asshole. He really didn't give a shit what he had done to people. Door number two was looking pretty certain. He started coughing up gouts of blood. His time was near. Turn out the lights, the party was over. Almost… His six-year-old niece walked into the hospital room with a child's curiosity. Why were none of the grown-ups in here with Uncle Davey? What are those beeping sounds coming from the thingies attached to Uncle Davey?

"Uncle Davey, are you okay? I love you," were the last words Dave Dow heard. Those words were a game changer.

In Hell's Admissions manuals those people like client Dave Dow are in the 40%, according to the book, 30% of all the humans you meet are just dumb shits who are willing to sell their souls no matter what you say to them. Then there's another 30% who will hold on to it no matter what promises are made, but the 40%, now that's where the real skill came in to play. If you have any talent, this is where a solid Soul Trader can earn his, her or its keep. Damien-ki Zakire Monteloflobe. Damien-ki, or simply D'mon to his friends, had been the top of Hell's Admissions Representatives for eons dating back to the dawning of man. Before that, he was prepared to do Soul Trading on other planets in other galaxies but being created on an Earthly portal, one from Jamaica Mon, so luckily for him the souls are plentiful, so they kept him on right where he grew up.

Damien-ki, was born in the Jamaican portal of Hell, which is a plane of existence with an appearance like that of Earth's Jamaica. The actual name of this world is unpronounceable in any form of earthly language (spoken or inscribed) only decipherable in Angelic scripture. Call it in Jamaican Hell for simplicity's sake. D'mon was born there and born a demon. He wasn't up there for the Fall that started it all. There is quite a difference between 'born' and 'fallen'. His parents, Quiroga and Bathsheeba Monteloflobe, were two of the original angels that fought alongside the Light bearer Lucifer and took part in his great Revolution and subsequent Fall from Grace. They were a part of the rebellion in Heaven from the get-go. Damien-ki heard stories of the balls it had taken to wage war against the Big G and Heaven itself and thus was proud to be a first generation, full-blooded demon born of such strong parentage. That his mother and father stood up to their creator seemed a badge of honor in his eyes. Coming from Fallen parents was to be descended from royalty. This lineage no doubt gave him confidence; however, his formidable skills were his own. He was a master of his trade, lineage or not.

Soul trading was a highly respected position in Hell, in many ways the corner stone to the whole operation, so that's where he went to earn his keep. However, like any great mind, over time he would be cursed with dissatisfaction. Bored and restless, Damien-ki was always reaching for more. The position of Soul Trader no longer thrilled him; rather he grew to hate it. He heartily despised everything about it and dreaded going in to work most days. Today was one of those days. He had made this industry his bitch. What more could he accomplish in an industry he had done everything in, except maybe get worse at it over time. Besting himself would be impossible. If keeping up record-setting numbers each and every day for the rest of infinity would be impressive however redundant. What else was there? What could he sink his teeth into next? What was around the celestial corner waiting to inspire him?

D'mon stared up at the giant pulsating penis before him. It was huge, huge and always fucking into the earth. Again, and again, its veiny shaft drove upwards into the top of the core driving its dickhead through molten lava and flowing rockslides. *Hell was an interesting place* he thought. Still, he'd done it all, there has to be more to see. He needed to see.

As he stood staring at his home for the next eight hours he was aware that behind him were creatures of all shapes and sizes, many too hideous to be named by human tongues, all dreamt up by man. Hell was not fire and Brimstone. It was fever nightmares come to life in a, shall we say, different plane of existence. Dreams, what a fun drawing board they were! The human mind, so creative and sinister! There were a lot of clowns and little people here in Hell. People are so scared of them. Silly, but fun to watch as the fear flew! There were a lot of impotent white guys, a ton of black guys with little dicks. Unicorns too for some reason. Leprechauns, which might sort of fall into the evil dwarf category. Tomato, tomaaaato as far as some idiots were concerned. Confessionals everywhere. The place was crawling with sixteenth century Cardinals and bell bottoms! Male pattern baldness too. Sometimes the demons were amused at just how silly human fears were. Unicorns! Really? Not as many rape type things going on as you might think. In some sick way that usually fell more into the 'weird girl fantasy' zone. Hell was indeed a marvelous place. Ironically there was a lot of science involved in explaining this bad religion place, but it would be a waste trying to explain it. Please do not take offense but even the smartest of humans are buffoons when it comes the ways of the Universe. It would be easier explaining how to use an iPhone to a flea.

"If they shudder about it in their nightmares then we give birth to it here." his mother used to say. Demons could readily change their shape if they felt the need depending on their clientele; however, most chose to pick one form and stick with it like a comfortable suit. Branding if you will. Their egos wanted to be remembered by their frightening countenances. Pride. Some of the beings were monstrous flesh-eating centipedes, loud screeching pseudo-dinosaurs, and bulbous fatty food ogres topped with piles of human waste while others were super villains or merely celebrity impersonators. Everything and everyone was interesting in some sort of nightmarish way. D'mon gingerly avoided a river of shit just to reach the sliding glass entrance to his office deep within the giant cock, all shiny pristine and sparkling clean inside. At first glance this office was normal. The purpose being to simply fuck with the souls waiting in the lobby. Waiting. Waiting was also a big element in people's nightmares. Hey, whatever works, right? Make 'em wait, they sure as shit weren't going anyplace anytime soon.

At the front desk sat the she-imp whores he despised. The front desk sluts were sisters and had no respect for themselves or the position, setting back women's lib by at least half a century on a good day. Shirley never made eye contact. Tonya was just a cunt. They both looked fairly normal in a sex kitten-secretary sort of way. It was the fangs in Tonya's vagina that snuck up on you. At last year's Xmas party D'mon had heard that 'Big Lips' Salisu found that out the hard way, pardon the pun. His demon-hood had grown back fairly quickly but like in any nightmare, not quickly enough. Cunt. D'mon faked a smile when he walked past the bitches in the lobby.

Yes, you read correctly, Hell does host Xmas parties. What a great marketing campaign that was. Hellish employees scuttle butted throughout the giant pulsating cock-building. The two secretaries were a horrible addition to the workforce, D'mon thought, and only kept their positions there because the President of the cock was having sex with both of them, sometimes on their desks during office hours. Such a lack of professionalism and decorum made D'mon positively ill. This *was* Hell after all.

President Duulexebub was sweaty even when it was cold out; his comb-over stuck greasily to his long curly goat horns and his belly was bulbous and quite pronounced making his suit always off kilter. His ties were seriously atrocious, but he loved his ties probably more than his ignorantly blissful nuclear family. The President was known for having a pencil mustache over a five o'clock shadow that almost reached up to his eyes. He would stroke it affectionately when speaking. The president of the giant cock office was married to a prestigious Hellion female and she had given the president two beautiful demonic children. Shirley and Tonya didn't give a shit. Maybe that's why D'mon was so very irritated by them, they reminded him of how much he didn't care. D'mon stopped outside the boss's office watching him flirt with another new hire. He was gliding his claws aRo her leathery brown breasts, flicking her nipple between thumb and forefinger. He noticed D'mon staring with a judgmental frown on his face and closed his door. Sure, this was Hell, but c'mon, have some respect. D'mon found it quite impossible look up to this man, as he was supposed to.

On his way to his office D'mon saw members of the Admissions team hustling about, some training newer hires about the standard ins and outs of sales, some waiting impatiently on leads by their Ouija boards. Each wanted to be the first to answer a call from an idiot thinking that they were talking to grandma or their new best friend that just so happens to be dead. 'Pathetic and stupid.' D'mon thought. D'mon smiled broadly revealing his handsome, sharp teeth, thinking of what ridiculous things he would make people spell out on their Ouija boards.

Is granny's soul inside the stray cat I've been feeding?
YES.
Is dad in Heaven?
NO.
Mom, why did you kill yourself?
I HATE COOKING.

The reactions from those stupid things used to be a laugh riot to D'mon but not anymore. Boring. He grinned in spite of himself. Idiots!

"I got him! I got him, seven-day lock! That fucker is mine!" A flame red scarfel exclaimed running from its office. A seven-day lock referred to the amount of days a soul has to change its mind. Once a deal is struck if the human decides to change their mind and burns the parchment contract before the seventh day then they got their soul back untouched by Hell's flickering flames and anal cavity searches. When this happens the soul trader doesn't get any credit and it was all a climatic waste of time. Whatever was agreed upon in the deal was nixed as well. No tickey, no washy.

So, for example, if a college kid pledges their immortal soul for a new car, then they will receive the car but if they renege on the deal that car will be lost in a terrible accident befitting the miserable fuckhead who wasted Hell's time. Fine print was a genius slicing curve-ball, but like red tape it could sometimes be made to strangle the pitcher or the catcher. Still, the Scarfel was ecstatic at getting this soul locked in as an official sales number for the month. End Zone dance! Woot, woot!

"Relax, it was a hardcore death metal rocker with pictures of his band in front of pentagrams, even *you* couldn't fuck that up," D'mon purred at the Scarfel.

D'mon was aware of the lead when it came in originally, Hell, he had passed on taking it on. Seeing how sad he made the scarfel with his comment (its flames lowered and went from orange-red to a light blue till finally its flames almost extinguished completely), should have made D'mon smile. No smile. Crap. So, to cheer up the little scarfel he muttered, "Hey, umm, congrats," and continued towards his office leaving the sad scarfel in the hallway, comforted by two other demons all the while giving D'mon dirty looks. D'mon knew it'd been wrong but dammit, he was just plain over this bullshit. Another soul, so what? How many had D'mon damned in his hundreds of years at it? What difference did it make? He was uninspired. That's a dangerous thing, very dangerous for a man, considerably more dangerous for a demon. Idle hands and all the jazz.

Our Demon hero found his way to his office and unlocked the

door with his key. The door was nothing special, its translucent glass had D'mon's name written around it in cheap black vinyl. Opening the door, he switched on his two fans, one under the desk and one aimed at his desk from the other side of the office. It was hot as Hell in there. The various nick-knacks cluttering his office carried with them an abundance of memories. Mrs. McElroy's stuffed Pomeranian, Tinkles, Calvin Runnels' sawed-off shotgun, Vincent Levesque's bowling trophy. D'mon sought meaning in everything. All of these things meant something to somebody.

Mrs. McElroy sold her soul so that Tinkles would survive her second round of Parvo treatments. Tinkles would have survived anyway but that dumb fuck old lady was a martyr and jumped on the grenade anyway. Calvin Runnel's shotgun participated in five successful bank robberies. Calvin was set for life, until that unsuspected Lymphoma got him two months later. Vinnie Levesque and his bowling trophy, oh, what a riot that was! What can I say, the fuckin' guy loved bowling and wanted to be the best in his shitty little bowling league in Bumblefuck VA, not the best in the world mind you just Bumblefuck VA!

They were reminders, triggers, bait. Tchotchkes looming out at him from every era man had to offer, some more valuable than others. For insistence, the two sticks Unnk used to create fire, as in the first mother fucker EVER to create fire just to clarify! D'mon was always amused by the memories and prestige these two simple sticks brought him. Every demon that walked into his office would stop and glance, giving homage to those two unassuming sticks. The fire was only meant to impress Gooma, she was quite a catch for her time, she had the most seductive sloping forehead and hint of chest hair. Gorgeous. Unnk wasn't the tallest or strongest but he was smart enough to know that he would have to sell his soul if he was to step out of his big handsome cousin's Cro-Magnon shadow. Not a bad feather in D'mon's cap, bagging Unnk. Best of the Rest 25,000 BC award was a biggy. He got loaded on Angelic ale that night. The stuff was contraband but who fucking cares seeing as what D'mon had accomplished that fine day. Behind him stood plenty of other awards, plaques, and crystals with his birth name and various accolades mixed with all his human keepsakes: King of Soul Catching/ England division 1890, Top Soul Trader 1867, 1868, 186. Napoleon's hat sat collecting dust on a hook to the left of the office door. D'mon remembered thinking it was pretty clever of him to promise that little French twerp fame in the pages of history and all he would have to do is have the balls to invade Russia. Russia, piece of cake, who did they ever beat? Sacre bleu! What a rube. On a side note, Nappy's hat was a tad bitter sweet because not a couple centuries later Zaffleburger, a fellow Soul Trader, would pretty much steal that exact same strategy and use it on a failed angry Austrian paperhanger by the name Adolph and the rest is history.

D'mon wasn't the only talent at the giant cock. Weelzebub was good. Loomis was good. Pee Wee Vee was good, but D'mon was the best. The best Soul Trader in the history of Hell.

The awards piled up, many more were still in their boxes left unopened in the corner, because none of it mattered. There was a Nobel Prize holding a stack of loose papers together, a glorified paper weight. It was only Einstein's. Fuck that no-name, Nicola Tesla. Fuck him and his altruistic electricity inventing soul. Where's his Nobel fucking Prize? D'mon took a long glance at Einstein's trophy followed by a short sad sigh. He then turned on his computer, or rather a bowl of blood with a keypad and mouse in front of it. You have 378,789,002 messages. For fuck's sake. He would be here forever. This was the only notion that curled a smile onto his withdrawn face. This was not a smile of joy mind you (yes Demons are encouraged to be joyful); this smile represented the nine to infinity work schedule D'mon had just punched in for.

"Hey superstar, 'The Fish Burner' wants to see you in his office."

"Yeah, in a moment," D'mon didn't even look up, he knew the voice.

It was Ray Ma Ching, the ADOA (Assistant Director of Admissions, over this Earthly Hell portal), Ray was a fucking fat opportunistic cherub from the Filipino portal (not like D'mon's portal from far away but rather the actual Filipino portal.

There was one for every universe, planet, country and city; two for the Big Apple, Las Vegas and L.A.) He hated D'mon's abilities since it came to him so damn easily and without much effort at all, unlike the rest of the team that read all the damn manuals and attended sales seminars in their futile attempts to be the best. The envy he felt was noticeable to many on the team. Due to Ray's best efforts in recent months many had begun to regard Ray as the better Soul Trader.

Ray was certainly not as gifted as D'mon, but he had a whole lot of '*gotta wanna*! In Ray's mind's eye al this was justified to the point of heroism but in all actuality, he was more crooked then a Kansas City Snake Oil Salesman. D'mon knew that this floating chubby cherub's official management position of power next only to Asag was what got him priority over many leads and especially the all-important walk-ins.

A *walk-in* is what Hell called those in the 30% that would sell their souls no matter what you say or do to them. An example might be a wannabe devil worshipper sitting in the middle of pentagram made from the blood of a cat mixed with his own masturbation spunk, while blaspheming about his God and making pledges aloud to the Dark Lord. Yeah, all that stuff is great, he thinks he's showing us how much he knows of the dark arts when in fact he is just showing the team how much he *doesn't* know, and how gullible this little puppy would be once they got their clutches on him.

"Not in a moment, Damein-ki, the Antichrist requests your presence now."

D'mon pushed his too comfortable chair back from his desk and stood up. The wicked little cherub fluttered in the air held up by its tiny leathery bat wings. They glared eye to eye, D'mon purposely holding the gaze long past the point that the fat little cherub pumped away sweating profusely. Finally, the little fatty couldn't pump its wings any longer, and dropped to the floor of D'mon's office in defeat. Now the confrontation went from eye to eye contact to something more like eye to waist. Ray squinted his little beady Kim Jong Il-ish eyes at D'mon even tighter than usual. Disdain was etched into his porky little countenance.

"Now that's the perfect height for you, Ray." D'mon smirked, "Don't worry, that's just a pocket calculator in my pocket, I am most definitely *not* happy to see you."

"We'll see how funny you are in front of Asag. Move it you." Ray ushered the large Soul Trading Demon out of the office. D'mon was tall and lanky with a hint of metallic purple in his skin. At first glance he had a Blackbelt Jones-Shaft sort of look to him; what appeared at first glance to be dreadlocks adorning his noble cranium were more like antennae on closer inspection. His tie had an odd kaleidoscope design and his navy-blue cotton shirt and beige corduroy slacks fit snuggly as though he had purchased them at Blaxploitation's R Us. D'mons eyes were shiny black with no white showing whatsoever. They were set deep in his skull protected by pronounced cheekbones and jutting, noble brow. Only the tiniest glimpse of smoky red light glowed deep within the Stygian blackness, giving those orbs a peculiarly animated look.

D'mon knew the way but didn't know why he was being called to the boss of Hell Admissions. Asag the Fish Burner usually gave D'mon room to do his own thing based on his sterling track record but lately that slack had dwindled as were his numbers of collected souls. D'mon's *'gotta wanna'* was fizzling at an exponential rate and everyone around him knew it. D'mon was well aware that he was fast becoming Asag's least favorite on the team. Least favorite on a team where the motto in Admissions was 'What have you done for me lately?' His *latelys* weren't that good and seemed to be getting more than a little bit worse.

'You feed the heavy hand the biggest share' was the excuse the former Directors of Admissions always gave in rewarding him with the most opportunities and leads above all other teammates. Nowadays that attitude had him getting more and more deeply into extremely hot water. D'mon let clients off not because he was going soft but because he was getting lazy. He just didn't give a shit. What was the meaning behind all this? Nothing. A perpetual practical joke on every Demon and angel within infinity? Was Asag in on this gag or falling prey to it like the rest? Okay you guys keep on bringing in souls because we, ummmmm, need them seemed to be the only mandate from above and below. These same gods and devils who doled out tasks to the blue-collar celestials who were responsible for building and destroying planets and knitting black holes into the cosmos, coming up with things like Spanish Inquisitions and huge fake silicone boobs but they needed souls?

"Why?" D'mon wondered idly. They must have built up these sad souls from whatever it was they used as fodder once upon a time, didn't they, before stuffing them into all those talking meat bags? It's not like God and Lucifer ordered them from eBay. Even if they had, they still created the guy that created eBay, so something just plain didn't fucking add up. What was the big fucking deal about souls and the business of acquiring them? Long ago, D'mon had decided that it was all just a titanic truckload of cosmic bullshit.

Ray and D'mon passed various offices and cubicles within the cock. Gordan Zxy wheeling and dealing on every phone his tentacles could hold, Slimey EggStax blowing her client, Jack, in front of his unfaithful wife who was chained down with her eyelids cut off and forced to watch. The office was all aflutter with good business. They could hear and smell the fiery temper tantrums of Asag in the distance; it rattled the corkboard ceiling tiles and quaked the floor beneath D'mon's feet.

Asag the Demon was known as the 'The Fish Burner' due to a symbol of his presence whereby the all bodies of water in his vicinity boiled over with such intensity that fish were burned alive and their little scaly bodies floated cooked and lifeless up to the bubbling surface. This could be a problem, especially with Hell's Corp image and dining at Red Lobster. A Director of Admissions on Hell's Sales Team also doubled as the Earthly incarnation of Evil itself, the 'Antichrist', so when Doomsday or Armageddon occurs the demon holding this position is in line to lead Hell's infernal attack on Earth. This mantel was a much sought-after position by those on the Admissions team. Something to strive for. Even the lowliest of the demonic horde had Aspirations to glory!

Ray and D'mon passed various offices and cubicles out of which shone the twisted pleased faces on the various Admissions Hellion underlings. The cock was indeed a big place filled with diverse professional areas such as Career Services, Financial Aid, Practical Witchcraft, Torturous Repossessions, etc. ZiggaZigAhh was a wizard at helping the deceased refinance their souls, this was a fairly new and innovative division here in the underworld. Something borrowed from the financial titans of the Earth. Her curly horns and large breasts offset only by her even larger thirst for souls was usually semi-orgasmic at the profit to be made from those fools. There were souls a-plenty for an intelligent and ambitious she-demon such as she. ZiggaZigAhh only stopped her wheeling and dealing long enough for a split second look up at the passing D'mon. The look was filled with the basest contempt.

Duff Beligowitz was another such asset-hungry demon, specializing in Career Services in this hellacious workforce. He stopped his machinations only long enough to snort his dripping wet piggy snout at D'mon. He delved back into his work, a smug smile on his fat face. ZiggaZigAhh and Duff Beligowitz, like many others, were more than excited to see the great Damien-ki Zakire Monteloflobe in trouble. The tiger fish in Duff Beligowitz's aquarium started to go belly up as the water instantly boiled. Fuck! D'mon realized that Asag must really be pissed; the phenomenon of boiling fish only occurred while Asag was angry or horny or, as frequently was the case, both.

"Thanks, fuckhead!" D'mon heard Duff Beligowitz's voice getting further and further away as he headed toward some new Hell.

D'mon knew that remark was directed at him and not at the Fish Burner, source of the boiled fish. D'mon searched his mind on what could possibly be the problem now. He'd purposely showed up late to miss the stand-up meeting, (a frequent and crucial ritual) but he'd done that before and never engaged the Fish Burner's wrath over it. Asag had never seemed to care one way or the other. He'd attended thousands of these meetings and knew the bullshit motivation spiel through and through.

Stand-up meetings were the way that a traditional day in the Hell Admissions office began. A meeting where all members of the team's most prestigious inner circle discussed and established daily/weekly/monthly goals and what appointments had been set for the day. For example, a demon might say when called upon, "Boss I have 3687 interviews scheduled, 1472 Souls for sure coming in (meaning they are at the end of the seven-day grace period), putting me at 4009 for the month on my goal of 6500 for the month!" Then they would be praised or threatened depending on how their numbers lined up. This is where they were told what a close family they were, not mentioning who had been fired or grilled alive the day before for missing quota. Last week Xen-boy was filleted alive whilst being sodomized with a chainsaw because his numbers sucked, yet all was quickly forgotten when Asag told a great joke about two Jews and a giraffe walking into a bar.

Ray was getting lost having fallen further behind as D'mon took larger and larger steps to avoid the robust cherub, eventually making it to the door of Asag's office a good few minutes before Ray, who hollered out, "You wait for your superior, D'mon!" The evil little fat man waddled as fast as he could but D'mon grinned,

"Can't hear you . . ." D'mon said as he opened the door, "You're much too far back."

Inside the office sat a slender reptilian bodied Cornthrob in a pretty violet dress. D'mon knew her from the Practical Witchcraft division but he couldn't think of her name right then. He liked her and thought they had a pleasant talk the other day, the one shining highlight of last week. Beyond her stood Asag, The Fish Burner, a militant Demon's Demon. The ceiling was high and vaulted because the Fish Burner was a monstrously giant creature who needed the space to stand fully upright. This massive red dragon was corner office material with a hard exterior. Deep down though, Asag had a softer side. D'mon had seen this softer side on many occasion, during a few of Hell's reward trips. Once over glasses of Quadren blood they had laughed, they had cried, and they had marveled at Vlad Tepes beautiful impalement art up close in the Boundary Zones between the many worlds. This was a brotherhood and whether D'mon wanted it or not Asag saw him as part of his Admission's family. Asag coughed and burped up a bit of fire. Cornthrob uncrossed and re-crossed her legs as if she was trying to tantalize Michael Douglas in a Nineteen Ninety's thriller. She wasn't wearing any panties either.

D'mon waved at the female Cornthrob whose name he couldn't remember. She looked away. D'mon waved at his boss. The boss did not wave back. Burp. Fire. Burpy cough. "Take a seat D'mon" Asag motioned to his clamshell seats in the center of the room. "Sure." D'mon said and as he sat, as an out of breath and sweating Ray Ma Ching bounded in the door. The cherub stood glaring with contempt at D'mon.

"Now that we are all here, Ray, could you please close the door?" Ray did as he was told and took a seat in an empty seat nearest the female. Asag sat next to D'mon. There was a stillness in the room, an uncomfortable palpable quiet as the female shifted in her seat. Finally, Asag spoke. "D'mon you owe Quanzaah an apology."

Quanzaah, that's the name!" D'mon exclaimed loudly ignoring what was asked of him. "Geez thank you it had slipped my mind Asag. Now what was that?"

Ray leaned forward, his many chins rolling over each other as he announced, "What you said to Quanzaah was reprehensible and it doesn't belong in this corporate environment. How dare you?" D'mon got the uneasy feeling in the room. Obviously, he'd done something really bad but he had absolutely no idea what. He looked at his boss dumbfounded. D'mon straightened his tie hoping it would somehow also adjust his memory.

"D'mon, do you need to hear it from her? Make her relive the incident?" Asag's fish in various aquariums began to boil, bubbles coming up. "Oh great, look what you did D'mon. Now Asag will be without his adorable fish until I have them replaced. Don't worry Fish Bur, er, Asag," The fat cherub's leathery little wings fluttered ineffectually as he made the most ridiculously sucky-uppy face towards the large red dragon. "Calm down sir, Ray Ma Ching will take care of everything."

D'mon was also getting pretty pissed off as he didn't appreciate being on trial without knowing what he had done to warrant this upbraiding. He felt surrounded and trapped in a place he didn't much care about anyway, so he looked the leggy female in the eyes and asked, "What dreadful thing have I done now to upset you, my queen?"

Quanzaah took a deep breath and stared at Ray.

"Go on," Ray said coaxing her to share, "You said I had a nice purple dress on."

D'mon remembered now. Yes, as part of the conversation they had he'd mentioned liking how the purple dress hung on her. *That's what this meeting was about, his compliment?* The Jamaican Demon's head hurt. He stroked his dreadlock antennae trying to ease the absurdity. It didn't help very much. "What does her dress have to do with her job, Mr. Monteloflobe?" Ray was defending her and at the same time enjoying getting a dig in at the greatest

Soul Trader in the history of his business. The little fucker was such a piece of shit.

Asag leaned his long red neck towards D'mon with his mouth open so wide D'mon could smell rotting flesh still wedged between those wicked sharp teeth from a meal eaten earlier. He spoke "D'mon you have acted inappropriately, and Miss Quanzaah is owed an apology."

"I thought females liked compliments!" D'mon said irritated at this whole mock jury.

"What the fuck…" Fish continued to boil alive in their tanks. Most fish that lived above on Earth cannot scream but the aquatic life in Hell is more ancient and their screams were heard load and clear in Asag's office. Various agents throughout the cock building clung to their desks and nuzzled keepsakes to their bosoms not sure if Asag would bring the entire place down in his fury. It had happened before. Lucky Hell had a great construction crew just in case any Angels decided to Pearl Harbor them or in case any upper management demons threw a tantrum. The office quaked danger-ously with the Fish Burner's wrath. D'mon noticed this shift as did the others. Far down the hall and three aisles over Duff Beligowitz tiger fish were now nothing more than over-done fish stew.

"I am sorry to have offended you. Won't happen again." D'mon said halfheartedly, thinking to himself he wouldn't talk to her again, ever. "We'll add this incident to the file that doesn't offi-cially exist just in case we need to revisit it." Ray warned while comforting the emotionally damaged reptile creature in the purple dress.

"See, Ray, as I said, it would be painless." Asag stood on his massive hind legs, his gold-flecked scales gleaming and rippling with powerful muscles and walked the apparently satisfied female out of the office. The large red dragon stared at her ass as she meandered down the hall to wherever it was she worked. Throwing a seductive smile over her shoulder, she swayed down the hall. She knew he wanted to tap that and she would let him soon enough.

She took her time and swung her hips a little more than usual because she knew exactly what Asag was looking at. Aside from being a woman and a demon, the leggy lady reptile literally had a pair eyes in the back of her brick like cunty head. Once she was gone the Fish Burner returned and slammed the door shut with an outstretched wing. Asag's long dragon nose and neck slithered thru the office, his large red body following.

"Do you know what kind of public relations nightmare that could have been if she went to HR on this? Huh? Do you?" Asag stepped on partially dead prehistoric fish that had been fried out of their homes and were now floundering about on the floor of the room. Asag picked up one of the burnt fishies and flicked it delicately into his mouth. The big red dragon stabbed a claw out to D'mon in an accusatory gesture. "What do you have to say for yourself?" D'mon looked at Ray who was smirking evilly, glad to be a witness to such an epic browbeating.

D'mon who was not willing to give even a modicum of satisfaction to the fat little fuck just accepted the situation with a shrug, "Hey Boss, I have paperwork to get too."

Clearly disappointed at this Ray looked expectantly at Asag, who just let out a big sigh and said, "Go on, but we'll discuss this again before the end of the day." Asag gave a fishy burp. D'mon had enough sales experience to know it could get real crazy here and the old bastard wouldn't remember this shit in an hour let alone by the end of the day. He could feel Ray's balls shrink with anger and the implosion of contempt within the little cherub. Ray was not a face-to-face confrontational kind of demon; he was gutless and conniving, a master of putting a metaphoric or literal shiv into your back from the shadows. D'mon smiled a big non-verbal 'FUCK OFF' to the pissed off fluttering cherub and left.

Back in his office sometime later D'mon did look at the stack of files and paperwork on his desk. *'Why so many damn files?'* He thought to himself. Not even his Nobel Prize was a heavy enough paperweight to keep these memos and contracts at bay. Why must everything be so goddamned difficult. But there they sat piling up, each kicked back from a different department for a missing piece of paperwork. No second human signature on the seven-day clause. No check-off sheet on the steps of protocol. No Hellion mission statement, etc. He glanced at an older memo that had suggested everyone change shape so they all came to work in a uniform: goat fur, cloven hooves, horns. Some white-collar idiot must have just watched A Mid Summer's Night Dream or something. D'mon crumpled it up then uncrumpled it. He just sat just staring at it for a second. Finally, he made a paper airplane out of the memo and launched it out into the hall.

D'mon looked past his office to the desk in the office aRo the hall from him. That had been Margie's office for more years than he'd known exactly. Margie had collected human skulls for each soul she collected upon their original owner's demise, her office had a thick wall of heads, some of these she had shrunken down in later years due to limited space. Margie finally retired last week. She got a brief 'party' with cake and a watch then she was hustled out the door and now her desk had some young fucker in it just getting her life started.

Stealing souls, D'mon thought to himself, *who's really stealing the souls?* This mechanical assembly line of a profession was using them up just as easily as if they were humans. The new recruit looked up from her desk, it was the scarfel from earlier, now with a fully fluffed up flame back over its twisty turny bodice. She waved at the great D'mon. No doubt longing to make friends and earn some pointers she could exploit. D'mon gave a fake thumb up sign and looked away from the Scarfel and back to his files. *What a waste of time!* he thought as he began to make the changes to the paperwork just to kill time. Yup, this run sheet definitely needs a happy face in a noose drawn on it. They all do.

The Ouija boards in every sales office lit up with a powerful orange light. This meant a human was trying to communicate. Different ring tones echoed throughout the cock building. D'mon's ring tone of choice was "Eye of the Tiger." In all offices sales reps jumped at the signal like starving piranha but not him. He just let it ring and heard as someone down the hall yell out that they'd gotten it. He couldn't possibly care less. He watched as a cockroach scurried out from one of the files. Its tiny legs carrying it as it hurried this way and that towards his garbage can. The files were kicked back primarily from the front desk whores, the president's unofficial concubines, Shirley and Tonya. When D'mon was first hired from the Jamaican Portal he'd complained about them to his boss at the time and nothing was done about them. Nothing. He was frustrated until he learned that unofficially Hell's Admissions was handled in a giant erection and controlled by another one, the President's. So many fresh conceptions and ideas that D'mon created were ignored because Asag was hipbone deep in demon vagina. Pussy trumps talent was a lesson quickly learned by the talented Soul Trader. Fish burned everywhere often due to the horny red dragon's libido rather than his temper. It was a daily occurrence. It was commonplace.

Fuck fuck fuck fuck fuck fuck fuck fuck fuck fuck fuck fuck fuck fuck fuck! D'mon thought at first. Idea after idea, memo after memo would go to waste usually winding up on the office floor pages stuck together with the Fish Burner's man mayonnaise. D'mon quickly learned to give ideas to Asag post bang session. Deliver ideas to Asag at that perfect moment just a few scant minutes after he had blown his load and was NOT thinking about demon sluts' pink parts. In fact, this strategy helped Asag avoid the inevitable and time-wasting cuddling! This played a big part in D'mon's success, over and above racking up souls like a champ, D'mon knew how and when to communicate with his boss. Politics! For fuck's sake.

"Um, sir, there's an Accountability meeting. They say you're next, D'mon" came a mouse-like voice. It served as a rude wakeup to his daydreaming. As he snoozed, leaning far back in his chair, D'mon watched the roach, eyes closing in bored turpitude. A fellow Admissions Rep let himself in to alert D'mon to the meeting. It was actually his neighbor from the other office, the fiery scarfel again. His voice was irritating with a hint of squeal, D'mon pretended to smile.

Accountability meetings were held once a week where the heads of each department caught up with you on how each department is being represented to your *clients*. Yes, Clients. That's how they were referred to. Damned souls being mined for power and profit, ultimately, they would most certainly be raped, molested, tortured or just painfully slaughtered repeatedly for all eternity. In this dark realm, these poor slobs were referred to as clients by these fake corporate zombies. Clients. The black presidents, failed Austrian paperhangers, rock n roll kings. Among the sales force from Hell these glittering examples of human depravity were known as 'whales'.

"Great," D'mon said knowing he didn't have much to report on. He just hadn't been working at all today. Not applying himself as his mother might have said. Sigh. Momma Monteloflobe, it had been forever and a day.

D'mon looked at the scarfel. "So, newbie, what is your name?"

"I'm Cruz, sir, and I'm a big fan."

D'mon had figured as much. He rose to head off to sector BF for the meeting and caught Cruz still in the doorway. "Cruz, welcome to the team."

"Sir, the meeting about the lady's dress."

"Fuckin hell, news travels fast. What about it?"

"Did you really, actually mean your apology? I heard you broke down in there, and that would be a shock to me…"

"Don't believe anything you hear, okay. You look like a nice kid. Truth is, of course I'd mean it. She's a dumb Cornthrob cunt and I said what they wanted to hear so I could get on with my fucking day. You'll learn what it takes to keep things moving," He cracked his knuckles then petted Tinkles.

Cruz just stared, so D'mon continued, "Like I said, welcome aboard. I'm rooting for ya buckaroo."

D'mon left the scarfel alone in the great soul trader's office with low flames again for the second time that day. He expected the Scarfel to swipe a tchotchke or two, after all this *was* Hell. D'mon wouldn't have cared either way. Cruz didn't even contemplate such a heinous lack of respect because he was that big of a fan. Tinkles, Napoleon's hat and everything else would be waiting there for D'mon tomorrow and the next day and the next.

The red dragon dwarfed everyone in the room, even the hippo-looking demon with the scar around his eye and the scorpion tail. Shirley and Tonya took shorthand notes the entire time capturing every word with hopes of spinning them into spiderweb spools of red tape sometime soon. The room got stuffier and the acrid stench of the cigar drooping out of Dewywart Cockerson's gob wasn't helping.

Decisions were to be made. Ray's fluffy cherub wings fanned some of the smoke away in little fussy spurts from his sensitive smarmy little fat face. The accountability meeting was a jester's court on the best of days and was crawling with various self-important department heads. Gizzle Grime from Torture Division was an especially creative task manager. He was a true genius at doling out repercussions to Hell's employees. He loved his job and it showed. Back in the day while he was still out in the field he had been a big influence on Thomas Cromwell who loved to push Cardinals into torching innocents in the name of religion. Gizzle would still be found singing, "I'm Henry the Eighth, I am, I am!" in the halls of Hell. Good ol' Gizzy's attendance at these meetings was never a good sign for someone that was in the hot seat like D'mon. D'mon should have been worried and possibly downright terrified and yet the elegant demon felt nothing in particular. He was uncaring and detached and they were very pissy about it.

Asag's grumbling turned into a fierce fart fireball. Asag spent the next unmeasured and endless amount of time lecturing D'mon.

He just stood there and took it with little choice. Ray hovered around the pontificating dragon almost like a back-up vocalist helping to beat all of Asag's points to death. Politics!

At a particularly high moment of frustration D'mon suggested, "Why don't you just fire me then?" Deafening silence filled the boardroom. Even the torturer extraordinaire was speechless, a rare thing indeed. Ray quickly landed on the boardroom table quickly folding his little leathery wings, so they would not sound like an attention-drawing freight train in the midst of this awkward, deafening hush. The, out of nowhere, they all laughed and cited this as one of the many, many reasons D'mon was so fucking amazingly great. Ray imploded with anger and contempt for the second time today! D'mon meant it, but the rest of the crew just plain didn't get it at all.

"Yeah." Everyone except D'mon and Ray laughed hysterically. This seemed to go on for a very long time. Fire from Asag's large red mouth cut the laughter like a knife. Again, there was deafening silence.

"Now for the real apology," says the Fish Burner, his red dragon wings flapping majestically. As it turned out, Cruz, the little flamer had turned D'mon in to Asag for what he said about the dumb shallow cunt as a bid for early advancement.

D'mon smile as the irony coursed through him. In a self-deprecating albeit motivational gesture to the fiery greenhorn, D'mon said, "You'll go far kid!" Cruz manipulated the situation, took it by the reins and made this situation his bitch. Politics 101. Fuck your opponents, fuck your constituents, fuck everyone, FUCK THE HAND THAT FEEDS YOUR SORRY ASS!

"Oh, there's one more thing," D'mon hauled off and he hit Cruz right in the middle of his fiery face! The hothead newbie crumbled like the gutless douchebag he was and that was that. Game over.

Quanzaah entered the room not sure what had just happened but hoping it was something to do with her and her evil pheromones. Ray fluttered next to her almost hiding behind her and said, "Now, D'mon, this time make the apology for real."

D'mon had enough of everything by this point, and he exploded. He began shouting, "This is all fucking ridiculous! Everything and everyone here is just ridiculous! Our mighty President is fucking the front desk girls." Asag motions for Quanzaah and then Ray (who at first hesitates) to leave them alone for a heart to heart. Asag belched a big, deep dragony sigh. Fire, burp. More fire.

Alone they talked. D'mon vented so much that he surprised himself at everything that had been pent up and churning deep inside him. "Fuck those memos, motherfuck Giz, all the leads these fuckin' idiots back stab each other for. Fighting for scraps. Those scraps aren't going anywhere. Those fuckin' scraps are there again and again every fucking day. Fuck Tonya, fuck Shirley. Fuck my Nobel Prize. It's all a god damned joke this whole fuckin' grind we're stuck in. This is Limbo, not Hell! I wanna make a fuckin' difference. Not bullshit. Fuck the walk-ins. Fuck the clients and even human souls!"

D'mon ranted, raved and paced back and forth, "Fuck you, Asag." Before D'mon could mentally edit what he was saying out loud or realize what he was doing he gave his boss a shove! *Fuck, fuck oh fuck! 'Did I just do that?* D'mon cursed his anger. This was followed by silence. A deafening silence.

Asag's large Dragon neck cocked back as if to position himself to breathe Hell fire all over the Jamaican-esque demon Soul Trader. Then, Asag, the Fish Burner, got it. There would be no fire breathing and there would be no BBQing D'mon today. Instead, the large red dragon leaned down delivering a great big hug to the stunned demon before him. *Whaaat*, D'mon thought to himself.

Then suddenly, making things even weirder for the Soul Trader, Asag started to cry. Big sopping wet Dragon tears all over D'mon. Asag was a very emotional creature and this was indeed an emotional moment where Asag in all of his infinite wisdom realized (or thought that he realized) just how innovative and passionate and ahead of his time this Soul Trader truly was.

"I believe in you, D'mon. I am humbled and flattered that you would reach out to me, your mentor, and share so much with me. I'm so proud of you and I want to see your talented head back in the game. You are destined for even greater things than you have already accomplished. Under my guidance you will achieve these new and wonderful things. I'm so thrilled that you have this powerful drive inside you and how I must have cultivated it I will never know, but rest assured I will continue to set you on the right path. You deserve a vacation, and after today I want you to pick a place to go to get away from all this pressure we've dumped on you." His large red paw leaned on D'mon's shoulder in a coach talking o his MVP pep-talk kind of way.

What was this fuckin lunatic talking about? The red dragon reached down to the skull-shaped speaker phone console at the head of the boardroom table. He smiled broadly and punched the line to his secretary. Asag called a quick standup meeting for all senior admissions reps.

No sooner had the Fish Burner sent the message than senior officers began gathering back in his office. The room now smelled like rotten eggs and hopeless soullessness.

Asag gave D'mon the latest walk-in in front of the team. "A drunken girl made an offer and is near death by way of a juicy suicide. Claim her for Hell and show us you still got it kid. The whole team wants to see you back in you old fighting form. Right guys?"

There were murmurs. Ray abstains with his fat little lips pursed like he just swallowed a lemon. Ray was pissed and wanted to say, "He'll just screw it up!" But, he kept silent. This was not the time. The fat cherub's little wings flapped fitfully with angst and ill-concealed disgust.

Her name is Jessica Ro and she just killed some naked asshole by accident then drank some industrial pipe cleaner shit. It is corroding her lungs and suffocating her as we speak. Asag saw it all. They all had, but even the Fish Burner had to be amused in that it was certainly not a typical way to off one's self. Her moments are fleeting. Fire, burp, fire.

"Well D'mon, what are you waiting for?"

Demon looked at the room full of idiots, all stealing souls while working at a job that stole their souls years ago. He knew he needed out. That vacation sounded good. He smiled and nodded.

THREE

In the still of the night, somewhere lost in the Mount Baldy mountains lay Jessica Ro choking as the sludge congealed in her lungs and throat. It is frightful to have the air removed from your lungs. You reach with your arms as if to pull a gulp of oxygen close to you hoping you can eat it, but that meal is a mirage. Her arms jerked terribly as her muscles seized from lack of oxygen. Life and sweat poured into a river of regret all around her. She could still see the dead man's nude body not far from hers. Zach was gone yet his eyes seemed to be fixed on her. He'd stopped twitching with muscle spasms a moment ago and she waited to be rid of this life, with its disappointments, lies and troubles including her recently committed homicide. The glue bubbled into her nose and the back of her throat. Jessica gagged with panic as the sticky glue formed to her insides.

Her pink birdhouse cabin door was cracked open and cool night air ran over Zach's body bringing his smell to her nose. Sandalwood and patchouli seemed good enough scents to go out on, it dampened the toxic industrial smell. Her tears did not thin out the mixture but rather added to the mess on her face. Jessica instinctually wiped at her jaw trying to push aside the goo making room for air. She only made it worse. Panic!

Drinking the poison was her choice but her most basic of animal instincts fought back tooth and nail. Her hands clawed at her throat without her even realizing it. She just wished everything had been different. She closed her eyes for what she was sure would be the last time.

There was a new smell in the room. This was ashes and soot, like a chimney being cleaned out. Jessica opened one eye. The air was still. Before her stood a roughly six-foot-tall, two-hundred-and-thirty-pound black man with dreadlocks wearing a mask on his face. The mask had horns protruding from it. Shakespearian in appearance, a deep-furrowed brow carved into it along with an ear to ear toothy Cheshire Cat grin. The mask seemed like it was made from Onyx, yet it moved as if alive. As the man behind the mask smiled, it smiled too. A black cloak hung from his shoulders making him look like an odd superhero. The voluminous black cloak hung past his shiny black pants and even shinier dress shoes. He looked at her lying there and smiled showing mostly polished white teeth but there was an occasional fang shining through the mouth hole as well. His eyes glowed with a blinding bright red and then dimmed into smoky darkness.

"You don't really want to die Jessica. Not like this."

"Am I dead? Holy shit, am I really fuckin' dead?" She forced words through her tears and goo-filled mouth, her pink lips caked with yellow congealing slime and bubbles.

"Some would say you died years ago, Jessica, but right now you are just, paused. Everything is on hold. Look at yourself in the mirror." He passed her a small hand mirror. The little mirror was pink of course as it was an intrinsic part of this pink bird cage which now seemed like a pink fucking jail cell.

"How do you know my . . . This is . . .! Why wouldn't?" She cut herself off as she answered her own questions before finishing them. The big man just smiled at her.

Jessica sat up and brought the mirror to her eyes. She'd instantly stopped choking and the vile cleaning product was completely gone. She could now breathe with ease unburdened. In the blink of an eye she was healed! It was a miracle, or whatever the demonic version of a miracle is. I'm not sure there is a word for that and if there is, then this writer pleads ignorance! The red-haired dreamer didn't know how to take this bizarre turn of events as she faced the masked man.

"I-I don't understand."

"Of course, you don't. You are paused like a video game, you might call it suspended animation, or whatever, for now as we converse. If you really want I can put things back, you probably had only a few seconds left of sand to pass through the hourglass of your tiny life in any case." The Soul Trader shrugged lackadaisically, "You made an offer and I am here to accept it. Simple."

She looked at him, blinking and confused, perhaps still light-headed from the epoxy blocking oxygen to her brain, she wondered if she heard him correctly, "An offer?"

"You said . . .," the Demon continued, as he rummaged inside the blackness of his flowing cloak. He poked around in that blacker than blackness with his right hand until he found a piece of parchment with frayed edges. He produced a rolled-up scroll. The scroll was just like one you would expect from a Roroad demon in a movie or TV show.

He read her words from it aloud. *"I would give anything to just be a success instead of a failure."* As the words were mouthed she heard it being said in her own voice like some parlor trick. He stood in silence for a moment letting everything digest. "So, Jessica, based on your own words, I don't think you're ready to go just yet, am I right? There's still too much adventure to be had in those old bones of yours."

"I was about to die. This is so fucking weird. Who are you?"

"I'm your new best friend, your new lease on life. I am Damien-ki Zakire Monteloflobe, but you can call me D'mon." On this he bowed and smiled his one-million-dollar salesman smile. She should have been scared or screamed like a girl in a horror movie, but she was simply stupefied. Real human reaction is sometimes not what you would expect, and this was unexpected to say the least.

She was tempted to cry some more and then scream a little, but something in this being's presence calmed her. A wave of confusing emotions washed over her. Trying to get a grip on a single coherent thought she did that fingernail teeth picky thing again not realizing that she was doing it. D'mon noticed, not saying or doing anything to acknowledge it but in his mind's eye he thought it was charming. Somehow, she felt safe and protected. "What do you want from me? I have nothing."

"That's not important right now, what is important is you." He sashayed his cape around to look moderately impressive. Why was he trying to look cool for her all of a sudden? That's weird… and why the fuck did he like her petite little ass? It was a detail that struck him, and he knew the devil was always in the details! The little things were the big things.

He pushed the thought from his demonic brain then proceeded to do a basic sales 101 manipulation trick whereby he asked Jessica about herself, basics such as her age, marital status, job, and what she wanted out of life. In her emotional state it all came tumbling out with little prodding. Once he had this information he told her who he was, albeit in a roundabout way using phrases like *'the other side'* in place of what he usually was thinking, *give us your soul, you, dumb bitch*. This bit of theatrics was much better for business. He then repeated the facts she related about herself using the same terminology as she did so that she would feel he had really listened, then upon asking if he understood her correctly, made a suggestion that perhaps he could help her. This was a process that D'mon could do in his sleep; he could interrogate, analyze and problem solve simultaneously, however in this instance he found himself taking longer, asking more than the usual amount of questions and just prolonged the conversation in general. His conscious self knew he was wasting time, but something deeper made him continue even after realizing that he had all the information he needed to complete his task.

Jessica was completely lost to his influence, she could see herself in the black shine of his onyx mask. D'mon went into another phase of the process, the 'True Life Roadmap.' Here he drew a large circle on the bare white wall of the cabin that had a numeral two in the center with an extended nail then he asked her to picture herself two years into the future. His voice was hypnotic; the sound of it crept softly into her ears. She was a moth being drawn to the flame of a future this strange man was propelling her to imagine.

"Life is great; you've sold millions of copies of your book. Tell me about life then, how would it be different?" As she spoke he added her comments to the picture with lines branching off from the circle. Their only audience was Zach's dead body. D'mon wouldn't let her get away with just saying 'new car or bigger house' he prodded for details, so it really seemed real to her. He painted a picture in her mind's eye of a life that had never been. After gathering all sorts of standard answers about love and happiness, charity and family, he put his hands over the circle in dramatic fashion. "But we're not there yet! There's a dead body behind you that you killed, and you could be gone too in a few moments so let's talk about life right now!" He drew a line and carved 'right now' just above it. She got emotional and as tears ran down her freckled cheeks he remembered the phrasing in the Hellion sales books, 'if they cry, they buy.' He had her. Once he'd probed for enough sadness, he drew a big arrow from the 'right now' section to the happy positive circle of 'two years from now' and asked her, "What will it take to turn this *girl* into this powerful *woman*?" His black soulless eyes twinkled with an extra red glow.

She looked up at him standing still in his dashing Demon wardrobe, while she sat naked Indian-style on the floor like a student in a macabre classroom. She had been broken and healed, broken and healed so many times in her life, more than he would ever know. Her desperation was intoxicating to him. He examined her from behind his onyx mask. Her pink nipples peeking out from underneath her round foreboding arms. Her slim waist heaved just to catch her breath and her wits. She pulled off the whole wounded deer thing quite exquisitely. He noticed that her red hair was the exact color red that people pictured the flames of Hell to be. He liked that. It intrigued him.

"I suppose the answer you are looking for, to connect me from the worst day of my life to a happily ever after, is to sell my soul to the devil. Am I right?" D'mon was taken aback at the directness. His lips pursed, and his eyebrows shifted upward, the onyx mask moved with him.

She continued, "On today of all days when asshole Derek is breaking my heart, I'm owing my friends all kinds of money, wanting desperately to be a success, hearing my ideas are shit from a rapist and then finally killing him and now trying to kill myself. You figure it's easy pickings, right? Well fuck you!" Her freckles were surprisingly still cute, even when she was mad. She was natural and exactly what a woman was supposed to be in his mind's eye. Shirley and Tonya were sexy and sleazy with fake heaving boobs and yet this meek little creature had him curious. Very curious indeed.

Jessica started throwing items from the dresser at the Demon who put his hands up. She shrieked and sobbed. "This is the worst day of my entire fucked up fucking life and I want to die. You are a liar and I don't believe you!"

D'mon lunged at her and held her arms as she screamed. He shushed her and petted her hair. "I hear you. I'm here to help you. Damn it, you called out to us, and we heard you. I'm here to make things better."

"Are you petting me? What do you want? My soul or you want me to suck your cock? Maybe kill again, this time for you? Or what?" Her breasts pushed up against D'mon as she squirmed. His focus was curiously distracted. She was warm in a way much different than hellfire. And she smelled very good.

"Your essence will be fine, thank you. In reward for a much better, well deserved life." Soul Traders are told to avoid using religious iconography in dialogues with a client. Never say 'soul' they have too many writings about it on earth. He tried to be comforting and reminded her of the things in her future wish circle. Mind fuck 101.

"What's with the mask? Are you supposed to be some kind of fucking superhero?"

"In some ways maybe I am. I do have some pretty cool powers. It's for the theatricality of it all, big showy bravado. You know." He sashayed his cape like before. She looked at him for a moment forgetting he had just apparently popped in from the Underworld.

Is this guy goofing off trying to be funny? She thought. He may have been trying too hard. Just for a second.

"Pomp and circumstance," She sighed. "This has been a horrible day." She ran her hands through her long red hair, gripping down onto her skull. The confusion racked her brain. The notion that most horror writers didn't actually experience a lot of what they wrote about was a given, they just made shit up and now she was actually living thru what was ironically the making of an award-winning horror story. Fuckin' irony!

"Horrible days, yes, I had one myself, at least you don't have a dress on for me to compliment."

"What's that?" she looked at him dumbfounded. She looked her petite body over. "I like being nude." Her eyes squinted at him like she was a little girl getting her proverbial pigtails pulled by a little boy from middle school.

"Its fine, never mind, I'm not here to judge you." D'mon released his grip on her and leaned back joining her seated on the floor of the cabin. They sighed in unison, both noticing and staring at each other with equal amounts of curiosity.

"You're here to claim my *essence* for Hell, and well, you can tell the Devil to fuck off, seriously."

"You don't even know Hell." He stretched his legs, rolling his feet in an almost childish way, very *un-demonlike.*

"I've read the reviews on Yelp, so, no thank you."

"Okay- you got me." D'mon raised his hands in the air a bit theatrically, "It's a bad deal for you. Maybe fifty good years in exchange for eternal damnation, but fuck it, honey, it may be your ultimate verdict to go there anyway so you could get a nice cool breather until then. I don't care." That was a lie, for some inexplicable reason he did indeed care. "Besides…" he continued. "You aren't the only one having a bad day." He took the masquerader's mask off his face, his dreadlocks falling in front of his eyes.

She stared at him. He stared at her. Silence… The seconds seemed like hours. The silence swiftly became comfortable (especially under the bizarre circumstances) what with her being visited by a demon just after murdering a dickhead and all that jazz. What pivotal thing would this demon say next? What cute desperate thing would the paused living dead girl say next? They both wondered. A few more seconds passed. Then…

She stuck her tongue out at him and made a raspberry at him.

"Ttttttttthhhhhhhhhppppptttfffff!!!" It was either the most childish or genius thing she could have uttered to the demon sitting beside her. Would the demon kill her for it? Had he killed for lesser offenses? She had no clue. A few more seconds inched past.

Then D'mon made the raspberry right back at her, "thhhhssspppptttttttt!!!" It wasn't the most articulate comeback, but it worked. He instantly felt human to her. He was mysterious and scary, yet he had a sense of humor hiding in there within him. Somehow this simple childish action and simple childish reaction created instant rapport between the two most unlike strangers. Simple.

"I understand being frustrated. Happens to the best of us. I look around and see things that just don't make sense at all, and I'm very good at making sense out of things. Sometimes I feel like the only sane one."

"Me too."

"When I'm here. When I'm down there. It's technically not down by the way. People believe in things they can't even see like God but they all go through the same shit with zero empathy or sympathy for others. I've never seen the guy and I work and live on a pretty flashy celestial plane and it is still hard for me to fathom that one dude built all this shit. How the meat suits hold so steadfast is beyond me. Sheep? Sheep! People are embarrassed and angry over the same things but never realize everyone else is in the same boat. War, impotence, self-esteem, peer pressure. Who wins on American Idol? Right down to stupid stuff. You honk your horn when people don't signal even though you do the same. Well it's like that in Hell too. I'm stuck here but I don't belong. Am I broken? Am I a genius? Maybe. Am I ahead of my time? Possibly. Any way you cut it, it's still the shits because I am stuck."

"Wow, me too. Ha wanna help me write my book?"

"Ha," He used his left foot to scratch his right calf. That made Jessica think of him as a giant cricket. She was amused that he had the confidence to laugh even if it was a brief laugh. She was under the assumption demons did not have any sort of sense of humor whatsoever. Her mistake.

"You know, I struggle to pay my rent, I hustle my ass off for everything I have. I know most people have gotten be in the same...

"Boat."

"Yeah, boat. But nobody gives a shit. Or they're too busy hustling too. Man, at least you are good at what you do. Well I am guessing you are. Are you?" D'mon looked at her without reply. He smiled, "Yeah, you are. I am buying your crap, creep.

"Ha! Well what do you know?" the demon chuckled again.

These little amusing giggles and sighs came more regularly out of both the dead horror writer and the Soul Trader as they continued to talk about nothing and everything. It very quickly didn't matter that she was in Limbo because he was keeping her company. They talked at length over serious and ridiculous things. How they both hated how pedestrians took their sweet ass time Roing the street as if it was the only time in their crappy lives other people had to wait on them. They were both baffled that there was a phone app that could identify different species of birds just by you taking a photo of it and yet world peace was just an unattainable pipedream. Time flew by as the two odd creatures talked. A young naked woman and a Jamaican looking demon… Hmmm.

The long and short was that they were both disgruntled with Hell and the job, both stuck firmly in worlds where neither of them felt like they belonged.

"What if I could fix this for you?" D'mon suddenly stopped talking about slutty Hellish secretaries and slo-mo pedestrians. His tone was different. She could hear his sincerity.

"With one wish."

She looked at him. She was staring into him, the real him, his soul, which is if he had one.

"Wait, what do you mean?

"Damn near eternal life, is what I mean," He was serious but not scary. Although, make no mistake, she should be scared shitless, "If… If I were to eat your soul," He paused, "I could give you eternal life. Well, until I'm smitten out by the hand of My Dark Lord. But in effect you'll live forever. I could quit. Stay here, I'd technically have a soul in me. I could take your soul with me."

"Where? What do you . . ."

She wasn't exactly sure what he meant. Was he speaking in tongues and riddles or maybe flat out lies? Was he telling the truth? Was this all part of the usual song and dance of stealing souls or was this something different? Was this something that wasn't supposed to happen? She was used to thinking of herself as different but not special. Did this demon really see something in her that she was oblivious to?

"Listen, if I were to quit Admissions . . . Hell's Admissions, I could get you past the whole process. But that would mean no more being a Soul Trader for me. We would sort of be out in the wild.

He explained to her how it worked. There is a process. "This has never been done before to my knowledge and it is unprecedented. I'm supposed to bring your soul back to Hell with me. You know, back to Hell. Your soul would be... deposited. Done deal. But..." He let out a big demonic sigh, "The period of soulless limbo is traditionally seven days. You have seven days to renege," he warned her truthfully abandoning the sales shit. "That's how it works in a nut shell. You... we would have a seven-day head start before any demon or anyone realized what was going on."

"We? Us?"

All this talk of soulless humans, slutty demon secretaries, and magical cell phone bird watching apps was overwhelming. Jessica felt like she was in kindergarten trying to take a senior year pop quiz Calculus exam. This idea about playing hooky with her soul was way above her pay grade.

"So, what'd you say? I take your soul, you live on now with a wish granted. I'm your fucking . . . whattaya call it? Genie, you got one wish, two if you count me getting rid of that other body and uhhh," D'mon pointing to Zach's naked corpse, ". . . and I never turn it in to Hell thus when you die it's released, no harm no foul. I'm just holding on to it for you. Promise."

"How do I know you're not lying right now?" She subconsciously put her hands over her heart as if that is where she kept that which the demon wanted. "You're a fucking Demon, admittedly!" Her demeanor changed from sweet to not so sweet.

"Fuck you then, go ahead and die. Your options are to die a

horribly painful death as a failure mourned by a few fellow talking apes or trust a manipulative soul-trading Demon from Hell that has billions of damned souls under his belt. That's the truth. Honestly I rather like this." D'mon felt unburdened being forthright but his demeanor too had changed, jumbling between annoyed and awkward. This was surprising to the Demon. He had noticed quite a few odd sensations since engaging in witty repartee' with this quirky girl.

He hopped up dusting himself off. He felt as though he should stand and look menacing or at least a tad authoritative. He practically spun around the pink cottage, way overdoing it. She watched him not sure if he was going to do something silly or kill her.

"I'm waiting," The demon said to the red-haired girl. "It is time."

Demon's eyes watched intently as the freckled white-skinned outline of the freckled white-skinned nudist paced back and forth. This quirky red-haired woman seemed like an angel with the moonlight glowing behind her (not something you would think a demon would regard fondly). She occasionally rubbed her throat where she knew much of the damage had happened. She was well aware that her self-inflicted injuries would return when the clock started ticking again. This frozen time out of time and place out of place where minutes had no business was a refuge for D'mon, he could think and breathe and relax. The Demon did not pace but stood his ground on the porch of the little pink cabin, tall trees staring down upon him without judgment. He too had anxiety but his was not of this world but rather concerned the possible repercussions should he go through with his plans to stay here. His calmness concealed what a great big cosmic deal this would be if she went along. No being had ever done that, overstaying its welcome on Earth; no Chasm, no Spectre, no Blazer, or even Midnight Echo had ever teased fate and incurred God's wrath by simply not leaving when its job was done. How would Hell react? How would Heaven react? How would the screaming entities in the unnamable realms react? This had never been done, not just here but not in any universe where any other Heaven and Hell governed. Beings that scraped on walls since the dawn of human time, all the while screaming to be let in, allowed but one glimpse of this all too human flesh put on such an elevated pedestal above others. That was as good or adventurous as it got, just a glimpse. Get in, do your job, get out.

There were words like 'Order' in both Heaven and Hell for a reason. What the ramifications to those reasons were rarely known because they were rarely felt. As a result, they were rarely broken. Yes, you could get filleted for slacking in Hell's sales force or have your wings hobbled in Heaven for trying to think for yourself, but those circumstances weren't anything a demon or an angel couldn't eventually bounce back from. The biggest whoop dee doo was the Great Fall or as the Devil liked to refer to it, 'When I Divorced That Cunt I Got Half'. But this… this was uncharted territory. Part of D'mon knew it was beyond treason even to think these thoughts and acting it out could be cause for an unholy war, perhaps tearing away placeholders and transitional leaders. Why, this could easily bring about the much talked about Armageddon, yet a very large part of him just didn't care. It wasn't undoable, just unthinkable. D'mon found it arrogant of God and the Devil to really leave the whole matter basically unguarded.

There were no armed check-in points or even swipe cards. Demons and Angels had their various tasks and that was that; do not deviate from the Path. It was supposed, like in the slave days, to let the slaves roam free without fences or what have you, because they just simply knew not to run. Well, if D'mon's hunch about Jessica was right, Mount Baldy might just be the opening to his personal Underground Railroad! Life in Hell was beyond boring and he wanted to shake things up. If he never saw another useless slutty demonic secretary or juicy lead again he would be just peachy. Good riddance, Ray Ma Ching, you fat stupid fuck! Asag, I'll see you and your over-cooked halibut later! Cruz, Gizzy,

Shirley, Tonya and Quanzaah and every fuckin' one else can suck it!

D'mon observed Jessica moving around inside the cabin. This little nudist could be just the key to the whole shooting match. He waited for her decision. D'mon's brain was racing. He was so used to being catatonically calm and lackadaisical, just not giving a shit and still outsmarting souls left, right and center. Yet, now he was overrun with possibilities. What was this excitement? It felt arousing getting his hopes up like this.

The eyes of the free-spirited nudist occasionally peeked at the Demon who was waiting for her answer on her porch. He knew that she knew he was waiting which amused him. The uncertainty of it all was intoxicating to both of them. He stood tall and proud, sure of himself. With the cape and mask off he was a regular-looking guy. Nude from the waist up, his dark skin had a sheen to it under the stars. He was halfway to being a nudist resort visitor himself. Without the concealing mask and cape, he looked to be a light-skinned black man, with full, sensual lips and long dread-locked hair. His muscles were well-defined, a jogger's physique. There were good trails in Hell. She snuck glimpses out the window, studying him. She wondered about him not having the fabled hooves, the devil tail. And what was with the lack of horns? If he hadn't kept her from dying she might not even believe his claims. There were so very many things that she was uncertain about. The Bible suddenly seemed like an elaborate fairy tale book, written to scare children and adults alike into complacent behavior. Of course, that's more or less what the 'Good Book' is but was its description of devils and monsters an exaggerated ruse? Were the things people were taught to believe in any denomination just ghost stories? This demon or whatever he was seemed nice enough she thought. Life was bullshit, maybe Heaven and Hell were too.

A demon was right there on her porch waiting for her answer. She could hear him leaning against the aging wooden porch as the railing creaked. He made sense to her; even the not so good parts.

She might be heading to damnation regardless of her decision, so she might as well get what she could before God or the Devil punched her in the vag for the rest of eternity. A demon that claimed to have her best interests at heart and who said that he would not deliver her soul to Hell but instead would hold onto it until he perished, giving her a near immortal existence was quite compelling in an odd sort of way. There was something in it for him too she realized. His feet, not hooves, simply got to stay grounded; a right human take for granted. It kinda made sense. Or did it? This was madness and what if the thing had lied and ran away with her soul once it was within its grasp? What then? Fuck sakes. Still Jessica didn't want to die. True, she had a moment of weakness after killing someone, but she meant everything she'd talked about with this creature, plus above all else she believed in her novel. It was a universe waiting to be created, her universe. Maybe that's how God created this place, finally getting around to sitting His big fat holy ass down and writing the eternal story. Only took him seven days. Well, perhaps six because didn't he supposedly rest on the seventh day, or something to that effect? It could be a success. It would be a success! She would be a success. Right then and there Jessica knew her answer. As she walked back towards D'mon he, too, knew her answer even before she could say it. It was the self-assured way her body moved. Why was he noticing her body so much, he wondered idly to himself?

She stepped out onto the little porch just short of the two steps leading to the trail from the cabin door. The air was sweet and warm as it blanketed her body. She looked up beyond the dead body and the Demon waiting patiently for her soul, to the twinkling stars above. D'mon followed her gaze. Crickets chirped somewhere off in the brush.

"When it is dark enough, you can see the stars," Jessica said.

"That's pretty."

"It's not mine. Ralph Waldo Emerson said it long before me; still I think the quote fits us now." Jessica looked at the Demon as its face looked away, eyes still on the sky. "Well, that's true in L.A. You know the lights block out everything because even at night its really bright. But you can always see the stars here and I just . . .," she was rambling, "If you don't hurt me, and you do make my dreams come true without damning me forever to Hell, how could that be bad?"

FOUR

"It's a deal then?" D'mon's face now turned to her, he knew her answer but he was just making sure.

"Are, ummm, 'kay wait one more thing. You're not gonna put some sneaky ass fine print in there where as soon as I get famous I'm gonna get hit by a bus or get A.I.D.S. spilled on me or something, right? Right?"

He wasn't going to dignify that with a response, just the slightest hint of a smile. She liked his smile.

Jessica nodded her head up and down in assent. He pulled the parchment out and laid it in front of her, then without warning stuck her left shoulder with a sharp pointed pen. "Jeeeez, asshole!" she said.

He ignored her and handed her the pen to sign the infernal document in her own blood. She grabbed it, her naked body covered with goose bumps from the prick on the shoulder.

"Some rituals stand the test of time, some don't, and just be happy that I've not yet asked you for your first-born child." She signed it, for a moment she considered signing 'Mickey Mouse, but ultimately she knew there was too much on the line to risk a joke. He *was* a demon after all, who knows how short his temper might be or how long his humor was.

"Now what?" she asked expecting lightning and smoke. She looked around then quickly back at him, trying not to miss anything. An elevator of fire perhaps? Magic carpet ride? Some ghost of Christmas future shit?

"Firstly, this contract is your *'Intent to Submit'* to us what is now yours. It'll be in limbo for seven days, which is required by God as your Grace Period. Typically, I would deliver this to the Hell's Admissions Team to hold until it is ripe but today I think I'll just swallow it." His black eyes surged with a red pulsing glow. He unhinged his jaw like a snake and swallowed it into the dark recesses of his ethereal body. She didn't run and scream but rather stood in disbelief; her eyebrows raised as 'holy shit' high as possible. Baffled. Once it was done he said, "That way it was never delivered, thus can never be acquired by those in Hell."

Jessica clapped her hands, jumped up and down then hugged him pressing her small bare bosom against his chest once again. Up close his breath smelled spicy. It was not distasteful, rather intense and powerfully impactful. It was sort of like getting splashed in the face by a crashing wave when you eat a stick of bubble gum in a TV commercial. She let go.

"What now? Are you going away? You're not gonna... you can't really go to, you know..." She pointed downwards, "Because then they'll want my stuff, right?

"Yeah. I mean no. I too have made a choice. I've decided that I'm not going back. I'm going to stay here." He took the cloak and opened it wide, the shimmering darkness looked watery like a lake at night. He threw the Devil mask into the darkness of the cloak. It disappeared into the other side somewhere like a black hole in space. He then spun the cloak on itself and with a push it all disappeared into itself in a blip. Then there he was without an exit plan.

The one thing he'd learned from Quanzaah in the Practical Witchcraft division, before he did the unthinkable and complimented her goddamned dress, was a loophole in Soul Trading. Having a soul inside you, even a soul of another being such as a client, makes you worthy to walk the planet. She never came right out and said it, but he put two and two together and began plotting this pipe dream right then. Well, Cane, stick a fork in Able and tell 'em he's done! D'mon would be the First Demon to be allowed (able) to walk amongst humans without a pause or appearing in a nightmare. He would get to experience just how genius that bird watching app thingy was first hand! He would get to experience so many things! Bubble gum flavored jellybeans. Netflix. Gluten-free edible panties. Having ball sweat. Everything! *'Sky's the limit'* D'mon laughed to himself, Demons often used that term sarcastically. Now he would actually live it.

"What about him? Zach, what about Zach?" Jessica looked at the body of her would be rapist still lying with his arm stretched out the cabin doorway.

"That's only a shell. Watch this. Ever heard of spontaneous human combustion?" D'mon whipped his dreadlocks over his shoulder so they were out of the way. He snapped his fingers and the body lit up in a controlled blaze. The flames danced like snakes from a Fakir's basket. Barely singeing the floor, it burned with flames licking high in the air. Jessica watched in horror as Zach's face flesh melted like bubbling cheese on skeletal bones. His hair burned away swiftly, a million tiny candle wicks. The dead man's eyes shriveled into black slimy coals leaving nothing behind but an empty charred pair of eye sockets. His tongue curled back as it boiled, then it too was dissolved entirely. His body made grotesque belching sounds as pockets of air escaped the cooking corpse.

Snap, crackle, pop! Jessica watched in revulsion and disbelief as Zach was deconstructed before her very eyes. D'mon had seen things that made this scene seem like a mild and mundane experience but Jessica on the other hand was a normal human who had only ever seen things like this in movies. She was a writer, a person that makes things up for a living, but this was real. She was living this. They tell writers to write about shat they know and have experienced. This had just been a whole lot of living in a single moment in time. The real life of it all tugged at the soul she would soon be without. The heat was so intense the bones turned to dust and vanished as well, swirling in little ash eddies in the evening breeze.

Jessica watched as all history of her deeds diminished to a smoldering black skid mark on the floor of the small pink birdhouse. Then the stillness changed, and she knew life continued again. The clock with the locomotive on its face confirmed it when the sounds of seconds ticking by began again. The clock was not pink, a white face, royal blue around with a yellow train. Jessica felt that the clock was in some way blasphemous to the pink hue of the rest of the cabin. If the clock was a travesty, then what was she for being a party to all of this? She looked at her Demon savior as if to ask *what now?*

"Now you write your hugely successful novel. Get to it." He motioned magically with his hands. This did absolutely nothing, but it made him look cool in her eyes. *Why the Hell was he showing off for this freckled human?* He was curious why he was acting this way. He had fornicated with plenty of Hellish whores in his time, but this was an entirely different feeling than lust, although lust was creeping around inside him somewhere biding its time. It had become common and typical for D'mon to have anal sex with very willing participants only to finish all over the breasts and inside the mouths of yet even more willing and hungry females in the heat of voracious albeit very average orgies when it came to The Underworld. Sex grew on trees.

D'mon could not remember the names of these faceless demonesses and human women with his semen glazed on their willing faces. He had sewn his oats since life crawled out from the primordial ooze, and it was indeed great, but he now desired more. Was there more? Lucinda Deflower was the closest creature from his past that D'mon could barely compare in any way with the redhead. They were both charming in unexpected ways. Lucinda had a sneaky way of tantalizing you, not so straight forwardly trashy as the women he usually encountered. She would whisper in his ear and vex his senses with ideas and suppositions. Jessica did not do this in the same way at all but his mind was intrigued by her quirkiness. Was this her being coy or naive? Did she do the cute teeth picky thing or purpose or was it harmlessly natural? Questions. Jessica and Lucinda both provoked questions. He liked that.

He could so easily answer a million questions for a million idiots negotiating futilely for and with their souls, but these two creatures actually created questions he would have to ponder. What an aphrodisiac that was. Now the big difference between Jessica and Lucinda was that the latter had millennia to hone her poker face and her game. Jessica was a babe in the woods and she had to simply be winging it. *How adorable,* the tall dark demon thought. She loved to write about gruesome things, she loved to be naked and unabashed with other souls, yet she was still an impressionable and sensitive beauty. She was so responsive to her feelings which was curious, and he admired her passion.

D'mon saw how enthusiastically she began to type away, her bare buttocks rocking back and forth on her pink seat at her pink desk. Jessica's long red hair caressed her arching back and D'mon found himself hypnotized by her. Her pale skin seemed like an abyss for his glowing red eyes to get lost in. The clicking of her keyboard keys and her fingers tapping at the mouse sounded like a song in Morse Code telling D'mon to listen and relax. Why was she so soothing to him? Damn? Damn it! Why damn it? Maybe it was a good thing? It'd been five hours and she'd barely taken a break. Motivated by knowing she couldn't fail and that every idea she captured would be read and adored by millions she strove on. She would be blessed or cursed to sign autographs while trying to eat in public. She couldn't wait. The Demon tourist left her to it and watched as the sun began to rise over the mountains. The stars faded into the ether.

He looked at his claw tips that he had used to draw the 'True Life Road Map' hours ago, but to his surprise they were now nails instead of claws, which easily chipped off at the touch leaving hands more resembling the human he was becoming. He turned his palms over before him examining both sides of his hands. As part of the change most of his powers would dim in the coming seven days before leaving him human in appearance although Demon underneath. This change was the stuff of myth, a very uncharted body of water. He would be swimming into the dark unknown. Would his change hurt? Would it be permanent? Would it effect his faculties? He was as smart as any demon ever was but would his evolution into a mortal man cause him to be as stupid or mean or naive as men were? Even brilliant men were monkeys in his eyes. Was D'mon destined to be like Unnk trying desperately to impress Gooma? These questions fluttered around in his demon brain, irritated bats around a belfry.

Once the sun was high enough other humans began milling about. He smelled breakfast being cooked and could see couples walking along quiant trails in the distance. D'mon looked forward to finding out what scrambled eggs actually tasted like. Eggs Benedict sounded moderately interesting. D'mon wondered idly whether the Benedict referred to the infamous Benedict Arnold, a soul he had personally damned many years ago. He would soon be able to decide if he liked his toast light or burnt, lathered in butter or dry.

He would get to find out how he would take his coffee or if he would even like coffee at all. Maybe he was an herb tea sort of demon. The idea of sunny side up chicken fetus was already sounding unpalatable. Fuck eggs. Maybe he would be a pancake guy? Orange juice sounded pretty inviting, nectar of whatever had a much more romanticized notion to it than something that was dispensed from a chicken's ass. Why would God create such a revolting creature? White feathered squawking beasts that pooped eggs. Maybe God was just fucking around when he came up with chickens or more than likely, God just did not exist as D'mon had told himself time and time again. He had never seen Him after all. Chickens. Retarded. He would now get to taste everything. He would and could see and investigate everything the world had to offer.

The Eiffel Tower amused him, and he had wanted to visit it again. He wasn't a fan of the cigarette smoke though. This was ironic, since Hell was full of it, or so people supposed. He liked the melodic sounds of French accents, plus he was fond of movies. He enjoyed the scene where Superman fought terrorists on the Eiffel Tower and saved that pain in the ass ingrate, Lois Lane from getting crushed in the falling elevator. D'mon heard from Asag once that BBQ was the shit! The Fish Burner could not say enough good things about it. Man, those human rednecks sure are awfully prideful about their BBQ and deservedly so! There was a little spot called The Pig in Memphis, TN, right smack in the middle of Beale Street where all the sinners hung out. It was a big party spot where, apparently, everybody sinned up an appetite and then gorged on succulent brisket and or pork amongst other delicacies. Stonehenge was on his list too, he was fascinated with the way that the alien architects had arranged those huge brooding stones. D'mon loved how it perplexed the human race. He watched the humans. All nude and not ashamed of their dumpy average to obese bodies. D'mon knew his dark pants and shiny shoes would have to go.

Jessica Ro came bounding out of the cabin and ran smack into a fully nude, formerly half-dressed Demon. She stopped dead in her tracks. She examined him in a way that if the roles had been reversed, would have been creepy and highly inappropriate.

"Hey you! I'm glad you joined the fun." For the first time she appeared devilish. Her grin was innocent and sinister all at once. Freckles. D'mon loved those freckles.

"Fun, yes, I believe this whole adventure will be quite a unique experience." He could see she was excited to share something with him. He found himself flexing his muscles. *Why was he flexing?* The freckles where responsible!

"Are you flexing?"

This comment caught D'mon o little off guard, "Uh, just stretching... This sensation is curious. I can feel the breeze blowing over me. It's making my skin quiver."

"It's done! I finished over sixty thousand words and it's not just a first draft; it's perfect! It needed to be over sixty thousand words because I want to get a 'best new writer' award from the *HHWAA, The Hollywood Horror Writers Association of America.* It's kind of always been my dream." She had beauty and brains wrapped in a delicate layer of naiveté. Her hair flowed like angel's wings which should not have resonated well with the demon but somehow it did.

"Of course, it is. I bet the book is pure magic. Tell me all about it." D'mon lightened up on the flexing, trying to morph into a more natural seeming pose.

"I can do better than that, why don't you just read it! 60,000 words!"

So, he did. The *Reversetronauts* was awesome! What an ingenious title. Hosehead was his favorite. He loved when Hoser turned back into a man just as he was biting the throat out of Casper Vaus the militant reverse vampire mercenary! The book was so authentic and true to detail not bullshit like so many writers who are scared of their own shadow. Jessica got to have the experience of committing murder and she put it to paper like a champ. She wrote as if possessed and she was! Hosehead was so torn up inside about literally tearing up Vaus. Hoser's inner demons were relentless and bombarded his thoughts. That's how it is for a justified murderer. Not a killer but rather someone who is forced by happenstance to do the wrong thing for the right reasons. D'mon was impressed with Jessica's fine prose.

If Hosehead wasn't genius enough, man, Johnny was a card and Ben was so melancholy; his secret crush on Sue was slowly killing him. This was fantastic. Jessica watched the demon read her novel. She watched his face, his expressions trying to decipher his thoughts. He looked engaged, was he laughing at her on the inside or was he really and truly impressed? How in the fuck could one not be impressed by the wily and dangerous blood-curdling adventures of Johnny, Ben, Sue, Richard and Hoser on a planet full of insatiable reverse vampires? Oceans of blood! Water spilling out of innocent veins! This God damned book had it all. At the end he told her that he loved it. It was funny, it would be scary to a human, and it was just a well-crafted little tale, perfect to put her on the map. People who read her words and be hooked. She would become a celebrity poet of gore and screamers. Jessica and D'mon exchanged glances as much as they did words. They really began to see who each other was, which surprised them both and both were more surprised that they didn't mind. The universe was a funny place and it did funny things like help creatures make these funny revelations; probably no thanks to God because the guy didn't exist. Right? Nobody had ever complimented her writing before, no teacher, no friend aside from Evelyn and even she'd probably been faking interest as a good friend would, but this Demon messenger of Hell had no reason to bullshit her.

"We make a good team," the demon announced. "I knew you could do it, Jessica."

"We?"

"Yes . . . we."

She stood there in front of him fully vulnerable, exposed, looked deep into his balmy black endless eyes and lost herself. One of his dreadlocks slid around his face as his head tilted examining her. She reached up and moved it not asking permission to touch him. He was a real-life Demon, was she allowed to touch him? If there were indeed rules about this sort of thing I think that it safe to safe D'mon and Jessica were both beyond listening to others and their fucking rules.

Two night and day different beings, yet exactly the same.

D'mon made no effort to keep her from touching his hair and face. Her fingers lingered there close to his eyes. He did not blink, not once. She could see herself in the red glow hiding deep in the blackness of his eyes. Her blue eyes were no match for his gaze. As her hand dropped she managed to caress as much of his chest and stomach as possible. It was not her being naïve or clumsy it was her reaching out and taking a chance. Her fingers lit up the demon as if her hands were on fire. The sensation jolted through his body with unexpected power. What was happening? Life was happening as the redheaded writer and renegade demon Soul Trader were both alive for the first time.

He kissed her gently, then harder. D'mon pulled away slightly, his bottom lip still touching hers. Jessica's lips begged for him to continue. Her soft panting was a thunderstorm in his brain. D'mon inhaled in a way that he had never done before. Their lips met again voraciously. They were intertwined. The demon could taste the peach from lotion she had bathed in, he could feel how soft she was, like warm porcelain. A demon and a human were not ever meant to touch like this but that couldn't stop them. Would the world crumble? Would Ray Ma Ching get to be head cheerleader as the Antichrist, Asag rained his Armageddon down on Earth for this transgression? Jesus could have beamed down with Jimmy Hendrix, Ghandi, and Ben Franklin and started a heavy metal band. Neither D'mon nor Jessica cared. That sweet, powerfully selfish kiss was all that there was in the universe in this very moment in time and no matter what it meant for the rest of existence, their lips would just not stop pressing into each other.

FIVE

"Jesus Fucking Christ! Are you really saying this to me right now? Motherfucker! Motherfucker! Mother fucking fucker fuck! Fuck!"

Every fish in any water source in a hundred-mile radius of Hell's Admissions offices, in the giant erect cock building, was boiled alive as soon as the words were uttered. The place smelled like a Chinatown dumpster at high noon. No tartar sauce to be found anywhere in this realm of Hell. Bodies of aquatic life of all shapes and of all sizes floated up to the surface in the living world alarming every creature and distracting from Hell's traditional life in the shadows. Lucifer would always giggle and repeat himself bragging about how his greatest trick was convincing man that he did not exist. However, on this day the Fish Burner would counteract that ruse by turning planet Earth into a red Lobster.

The news stations reported strange incidents of fish boiling and surfacing belly up. The Vatican had a field day with the phenomena. Cardinal Nicholas Ciampi would one day write a best seller about this day (and he would write it without a Hellish contract unlike a certain nudist horror writer). The large red Dragon flailed his limbs and swished his wings violently. Fuck. Such anger and annoyance raged from every pore on Asag, the Fish Burner's body, and was to be a legendary outburst recorded in writings for eons to come. One tenth of the aquatic life on Earth died that day. This, the seventh and last day of the grace period from which Jessica Ro was eligible to repossess her soul from her devilish agreement. This day would go down in history as the infamous *Fish Fry*. The contract between the redheaded writer and Hell was now infernally binding and celestially valid yet there was no delivery, no explanation, no nothing!

Zatorg Bah, Suckszzy Die and AuZ stood in fear (trying their best to contain themselves) watching the huge pissed off red dragon. The three members of the Transport Council stood in The Fish Burner's executive corner office; three very different yet equally disturbing creatures. Zatorg Bah was a handsome East Indian looking man from the waist up but endowed with scorpion legs and a bunny tail. He was the newest member of the TC. Suckszzy Die (or better known as Mr. Die) was a Charon-lookalike pimp with a skull face, leopard skin grim reaper-ish silk bathrobe and heavily laden with more gold necklaces than 27 Mr. Ts! The senior TC member, AuZ was a scrawny, filthy clown with elephant tusks and a giraffe neck. The strange animalistic clown was nervously explaining what had become of D'mon. The odd clown was especially nervous as he knew that this could mean his demise at any moment whether it was his fault or not. He was usually praised for his attention to detail hence his name 'A-to-Z'. They reported that D'mon's cloak and mask had come through on a return but without the demon attached.

"Fuuuuuuck," Asag let out a fiery burp.

This could mean a multitude of explanations, either he'd been attacked and killed which would be likely to cause a war, or is being held ransom, also likely to cause a war, or possibly (and this was Asag's least favorite suggestion), he had gone AWOL, running from his duties and obligations in Hades, which when news got out was likely to cause a celestial war and a civil war and a religious war and every other kind of fucking war you can think of. None of this was good news, wars cause many casualties and Asag knew that he had someone to answer to just like everyone else but while D'mon could manipulate his boss Asag, the truth was that The Fish Burner knew his boss was not so easily swayed. He alone answered directly to Old Scratch himself, Lucifer, the Prince of Demons and Master of Hell itself.

The Morning Star was a magnificent ruler in Hell. He ran things with an iron fist garbed in a satin glove as Napoleon had put it (they were regular golf partners). He was as mean they come but he was fun and stylish about it. Theatrical and raw was an understatement when it came to the fallen angel. Lucifer was beyond drama and petty games, there was a chance The Dark Lord might destroy Asag immediately or do even worse than that. Death by sawing was one of Lucifer's favorites. He had made it popular during the Roman Empire; an oldie but a goodie, and the first half of the first century AD was one the Devil's most cherished times. Would that be Asag's fate? Or would Lucifer punish him in a more contemporary way, would He make the Fish Burner watch an eternity of Reality TV? Be it the *death by sawing* or the *death by House Wives of Cincinnati,* either way or whatever way Lucifer would choose as punishment for Asag it was definitely going to suck ass. Asag's only chance was to get ahead of the unprecedented catastrophe and stop it before the news reached his Dark Lord. Time would be of the essence seeing as the Lake of Fire was already marinating in gossip and rumor. That was a meeting he would put off for as long as he had to. The Devil has eyes and ears everywhere. It would be only a matter of time before the news of this infernal fuck up made its way to Lucifer's pointed furry ears, should he choose to have such things.

Ray Ma Ching floated about fitfully as Asag addressed the

news. Hell was crawling with whispers of confusion all around them.

"So, he's just gone? Gone, gone, gone." Asag's neck bubbled up with rage, veins pulsing. Finally, he let loose with a scream of frustration, anger, and a dash of fear for his own future. A large underwater dinosaur threw itself out of the scolding hot water and lay dying on the floor. Rather than save it, Asag jumped on top of it and pounded it into mush with his large red dragon fists. Vile green sludge sputtered from the beast accidentally bukake-ing Ray Ma Ching. The Asian Cherub wiped the goo from his already squinty little eyes in revulsion. All those witnessing it waited for the moment to pass. Ray dared not say a word. Asag vomited fire and roared like a mindless beast; he pounded on his desk obliterating it and decapitated the mail boy who just wandered in to deliver the last stack of mail he would ever deliver. Finally, the Fish Burner stood and wiped the evidence of the fish murder and mail boy murder on a handkerchief Ray thoughtfully handed him. If Ray wasn't hovering around like a big fat evil bumblebee it very well might have been he that was suddenly without a head. The handkerchief had Asag's Initials on it and had it not been smeared with fish goo might be very classy.

"We had no reason to suspect anything out of the ordinary your Antichrist'iness. Souls get misplaced or damaged here and there. It is rare, but this is a business that usually runs quite smoothly." AuZ gulped, wishing he hasn't just said the thing about business running smoothly as it was an invitation to his own death. "D'mon has dawdled before so nothing new. We never really think twice about it because his numbers are like no other, so we just figured that was his way and if it ain't broke don't fix it." Again, he thought to himself, *why the fuck did I just say that shit.'* Another giant gulp of fear rolled uncomfortably down his long giraffe neck.

"He could be anywhere. The lead's soul could be anywhere. We are usually given some various forms of tracking the soul, but things seem to be quite out of order." Mr. Die interjected. *Thank God another demon was saying something stupid.* AuZ thought.

"There is no protocol for this, Asag. There didn't seem to be any reason or cause for alarm seeing as how it is an unthinkable and impossible situation. No demon in their right mind would think to act on what is unfolding before us. Why would any demon want to willingly be amongst the walking talking apes? This is just so bizarre and disgusting. Real life, ewwwwwww." AuZ' clown face was genuinely baffled and Asag could sense his sincerity, which did nothing to stop the Fish Burner from biting off his head leaving a flailing bloody giraffe neck attached to a convulsing body. The demonic clown body ran around the room for a moment not realizing it was dead like an unlucky chicken meeting the farmer's axe. Before the body had the good sense to drop, it was, like the dinosaur fish, char-broiled by the red dragon's breath until it was nothing more than ashes swirling in the wind.

"I'm going to ask that you gentlemen keep this under your hats for the time being until I figure this shit out, okay?" The Transport Council of Three (make that now TWO) looked back and forth from each other to the headless dead fish, and finally to a considerably calmer Asag before one of them had the courage to speak up.

"Seven days is our standard money-back guarantee period. There was no reason to suspect any foul play from D'mon or anyone involved in dispatching him. Seven days is not that big of a head start to get to the point of being unreachable. Earth is not that big, just the vilest." Mr. Die made a good point. Where other, larger Hells (in the geographic sense) governing other larger worlds throughout the universe had a size advantage, when it came to sin, Earth was flourishing with both quality *and* quantity. God bless the Spanish Inquisition, A.I.D.S, Cancer and 911... What a riot!

"D'mon has had a head start to hide from us for seven fucking days?" the red dragon seethed. "I want to know why, how, who, where and what is behind this folly! Whether this was D'mon's own doing or not I, want answers YESTERDAY!" The red Dragon turned the oozing mess that used to be a giant pre-historic looking fish and coated it with fire from his long red mouth until it was nothing but black soot on the floor. He did not want to accept that this was most likely D'mon's doing, but his common sense was tingling, "Was this anarchy, insubordination, kidnap or murder? Get to the bottom of this mystery before I erase the lot of you!"

"Understood Antichrist, we lay the issue at your feet. As always, with much respect." Ray knew just when to chime in. The fat little fucker was a world-class ass-kisser. Droplets of slime singed as they fell from the soaked Asian cherub as they hit the smoldering floor of the Fish Burner's office.

"I appreciate that, Ray. Leave me."

The remaining two TC members were only too happy to get the fuck outta Dodge.

When Asag was finally alone with Ray, the big red dragon slumped back in his large fanciful chair and lamented. "I have a meeting with the High Council of the Underworld in moments. You know that I can't bring this up. 'Hello Council, oh, how are things in Earth's Hell? Well, gee, we could use more fish in the tanks, new hires in sector 2, and I fucking lost a goddamn Demon to the mortal world!' Sure, that'll go over goddamn titty sucking motherfucking cock-biting well now won't it you fucking fool? I'll sink like a rock to the bottomless pits of the Lake of Fire for that. Torn apart by a thousand ratigans because I didn't just lose an Executive Admissions Representative, I lost one known to all as the top Soul Trader in the history of this Hell, dooming more souls than any other, a guy all teams in all worlds would gladly make their MVP, is just missing. Poof!" Asag looked balefully at Ray Ma Ching for answers or suggestions. The fat little Asian portal cherub fluttered about chewing his bottom lip, shrugging.

Ray's head was full of ideas but not to save his boss's ass. Ray was an opportunistic D-Bag and saw himself as the rightful Director of Hell Admissions which would ultimately lead to his reign as historical Antichrist on Earth in times of the End of Days. Ray knew that D'mon disappearance could aid in that pursuit but not until he found out what had happened to him. Ray worked hard as far as he was concerned, of course the evil little cherub also counted shady politics and manipulation as work.

"We need to find him, see what the situation is." Burp. Fire.

"Agreed. I'll send an Echo at once, maybe two Echoes if we need to." Ray sounded so happy to help the red dragon but lamented about him deep on the inside. *Fuck you Asag, just fuck you,* the chubby Asian demon thought to himself.

"Director, as your Assistant I feel responsible. I should have spoken to him before he left, we all saw signs that he was cracking under the pressure and I feel horrible as his direct supervisor that I didn't stop it." His little wings fluttered, "I thought his workload was a lot, but it wasn't anything that I personally couldn't handle so I naturally assumed that so could he. Maybe sometimes I'm guilty of seeing the best in a demon's potential. Maybe I am guilty of assuming they love this job as much as I do." The fat little puti sighed theatrically for emphasis.

Asag considered this, scratching himself with his wing.

"Please allow me to go. I'll find him, and I'll return with answers on this most egregious error." Ray was practically an angel… if angels were poisonous little assholes.

"You want to go?" Sigh.

"Asag, I owe you that much, let me try to bring him back, or just sweep it away like it never happened, boss." Ray practically had a red nimbus glowing around his head, a saintly Demon, Asag's new shining champion.

The wall to Asag's left lit up in fire that seemed to dance with a mind of its own. This was the invitation to the High Council meeting. Hellion flames rose and fell awaiting Asag, the Fish Burner, to join it.

"Alright, catch up with the Transport Council, and Ray, please don't let me down. Our reign at the top of the food chain here in our infernal abode is at risk. Don't forget that."

"Understood Sir," Ray bowed dramatically whilst fluttering in the Hellish ether.

Once Asag had stepped through the flames and had vanished, leaving an unscarred office wall with a motivational poster on it, Ray walked over to the desk. He jumped up onto the gigantic seat, his tiny bum barely making a mark, a single child in a bouncy castle, he put his stubby little pig feet up on the desk then laughed for quite an elongated while. The Asian angel reached forward and took one of The Fish Burner's business cards and wrote on it in black magic marker: RAY MA CHING - ANTICHRIST. He sat back eyeing its look on the desk and grinned a small fanged smile.

"Your reign, is at risk, 'Fish Burner', but mine hasn't even begun . . . yet." Ray's ominous laughter came bubbling back for an encore. Souls being tortured throughout Hell this minute would feel an extra jolt of pain in their various agonies as a side effect of the Antichrist runner up's happiness as it screamed around the underworld.

Evelyn watched as the two nude bodies walked along the path leading from the pink colored birdhouse cabins towards the 'Y' which split the path into a pair of trails, one leading to the recreation areas and one leading off to distant trails for nude hiking. She paid attention to the black man's demeanor and to the white-skinned, red-haired woman's body language. Jessica tugged at the pink towel on her shoulder as she laughed and smiled at him. After a brief hug they parted ways with him disappearing into the hills and her coming closer toward where Evelyn sat. Evelyn smiled letting the python tangle and weave its way around her body as she sipped her lemonade from a green plastic tumbler.

Jessica noticed her friend and smiled back. She laid out her pink towel nearby to collect some sun on the grass.

"You missed yoga this morning," Evelyn spoke in baby talk, petting her Burmese. Her large middle-aged left breast rose as her snake slithered around her belly and ribs hoisting the boob upward. As the snake crept up her back the women's breast fell back into its originally semi-sagging place.

"How was the turnout?" Jessica tried to sound interested and apologetic while see observed the serpent's green and brown scales shimmering under the heavenly sunlight.

"Well, it's always more in the summer but we had probably seven bodies. You know how it is, mostly men, but two couples which was nice. Have you seen Zach? His wife was asking about him."

"His wife? Ah, nope." Jessica shook her head thinking, *Oh, you mean Rapey McRaperson?* How far away that seemed to her. Everything that had happened to her in the last few hours dwarfed the murder of the philandering grip to a minor blip in her life radar. She sighed then smile broadly. "I finished my novel."

"What? Is it a children's book? How did you do it so darn fast?" She blew kisses at the snake looking back and forth between the cuddly reptile and her naked guest.

Jessica giggled at the idea. "*Reversetronautsis* isn't a kid's book, " she was mesmerized by how the snake moved, how it used Evelyn's body as its own personal set of monkey bars.

"Nakey and I would love to give it a read," Evelyn said stroking the snake's head gently. "Wouldn't we darling?" The large Burmese turtled its head ever so slightly at the touch of her fingers then extend it again tasting the air with its tongue.

"I was inspired. I found my muse." A sunny youthful smile washed over her freckled face.

"Is it a certain well-endowed black gentleman?" The older lady swung her hips back and forth with Nakey's tail swinging between her legs; a make shift penis.

"Evelyn! I can't believe you," her blushing cheeks camouflaged her freckles as she giggled.

"It is huh? Tell me about him. Like for starters how did he get in here?" She raised an eyebrow in a pretend mad sort of way. "We don't have him registered at the front as a guest. That's not too good." The snake hissed just then as if trying to be a part of the conversation. Nakey seemed to be wanting to get his two cents in.

"His name is . . . Damon, and he's not from around here. He's from . . . Jamaica. He got lost and I found him."

"Did you 'find' him all night long?"

"Eeeeeveeeelyyynnnnn!"

"You have to be careful. One time I got caught up with a bad guy and in some ways, I'm still paying the price for it." Evelyn offered Jessica an apple she took from the green fruit bowl between them on the grass.

"So, you see it's important that I have a talk with him one on one for Guest Relations comfort and all. Maybe tomorrow he and I can go for a ride in my helicopter. I've renamed my Nudie-copter." The Burmese continued to wrap itself around Evelyn and she willingly cooperated. Evelyn bore the large sinuous creature with seemingly very little effort. It was hard for Jessica to guess just how long Nakey was in his coiled state, but she knew that Burmese Pythons were one of the largest and longest snakes in existence thanks to endless hours of watching National Geographic. The patterns on the reptiles back vaguely resembled skulls. It seemed odd to Jessica that she hadn't noticed this until just this very moment. It was almost as thought the snake had morphed its patterning when she wasn't looking. Weird. Very weird indeed.

"Cool, I'll let him know. Hey, Nakey usually is a good judge of character what does he say about my new friend?" Jessica said daring to stroke its skully scales and then quickly retracted her hand. Evelyn looked at her with a dead serious look.

"Nakey doesn't like him being here, he says he's a bad boy and is wanted back home, right away."

D'mon at first walked, then jogged, then ran, then sprinted as fast as he could up the hills with sunshine warming his nude ebony human flesh. The droplets of his sweat felt like a million little creatures scurrying around his new exterior. Wearing only the dress shoes and black socks that were now only mementos of his time working in Hell,

D'mon enjoyed the peculiar fiery sensation of his lungs pumping with real oxygen. He was very definitely enjoying testing the limits of this new skin suit shell that he wore. Rocks and dust kicked up in clouds all around him as he huffed and puffed his way along the dirt trail for three whole miles. His throat got dry and he slowed to a light jog again. He looked around at nature's beauty that spread out before him. His eyes were no longer black with an inner red glow, now new blue irises gleamed, and his pupils contracted to restrict the intake of sunlight. Seeing a stream of water, he stopped and scooped up some in his hands and brought it to his face. The coolness ran along his contours and he liked the feeling of it. In the distance he saw the mountains and some wild burros further on. The former demon reached back down and let another splash of water come from his hands to his face, but it never came. D'mon opened his eyes and saw that the water was suspended in air. Droplets fixed in place, he turned to look at the trees which no longer swayed in the breeze or had leaves fall, all was still, and all was in a pause.

D'mon, from his place on his knees, where he knelt to gather water from the stream, saw a fluttery cherub rising above it reflected in the still frozen stream.

"Damein-ki . . . Damien-ki Zakire Monteloflobe, it is you. Unharmed I gather, aside from the pains of a morning jog, yes?"

"Yes, Ray," his disdain for Ray had always been tempered by his indifference and he could see the little jerk coming a mile away. This new human version of disdain filled D'mon swiftly and unexpectedly. The former Soul Trader did not like his former supervisor being able to sneak up on him as he had just done.

"Well, everyone who's anyone is in a bit of a tizzy about the loss of YOU. You're a pretty important fella to lose. So, what happened down here, be straight with me. Who kidnapped you?" Helen Keller could have seen and heard the condescension in the Asian cherub's tone. "Where's the soul? Why didn't you return? You didn't fall in love, did you? How cliché."

D'mon stood up abruptly. The floating paused water pushed away from him. Ray stumbled and back peddled into the air making room for the former employee of Hell. D'mon practically swung at the Asian cherub with his exposed reproductive hardware. Ray eeked out a less than attractive whiney gurgle then an equally unattractive snort. Ray did not like that D'mon was tall and handsome or at least taller and more handsome then himself. Ray saw himself in all of his pudgy piggish glory as quite a looker.

"No, nothing like that, rather I fell out of love with sales, and Hell. I'm not going back, Ray."

The cherub fluttered about kicking at the air. He couldn't believe his good fortune. He rested his feel on the stilled water. He walked on it as though it was a hardwood floor. With a laugh that could kill flowers, the little demon, Ray Ma Ching hummed and chirped towards the sky.

"Ya know, Damein-ki, I do like you."

D'mon looked at him quizzically, scratching his balls more as a statement then due to itchiness.

"No, no, I do. I've always wished I could be like *you*, the process always came so easy to you. I respect that. You've racked up numbers like nobody else. You know Asag sent me to talk with you… to see if you were alive, see how you are." He snorted, "So tell me, how are you?"

"I'm great, Ray, better than I've been in a hundred years and I'm not interested in going back no matter what you say or offer.

I'll blend in here with these walking batteries and keep the answers of life's secrets and their mortality to myself."

Ray welled up with hate. His chubby insides burned with envy and contempt. He hated that D'mon, even now, didn't consider him as a threat.

"If you took her soul and you aren't returning it to Hell, then my friend, that is theft and that puts you in hot water with Asag. You don't want to be in that deep end, ask the fishes."

D'mon paced, he knew this was true.

"Unless I go to bat for you. Put in a good word. He encouraged you to take a vacation, right? Well a demon has never taken a pleasure tour of Earth before. That could prove useful in collecting data. Tell you what, pal, I'll see what I can do with Asag. He was very upset, but I know he has always been quite inordinately fond of you."

D'mon was pleased at this.

"I could pitch it like this was a surprise from you to the Fish Burner. You showing the initiative that he knows you have within you but has been dormant of late. You are reawakening that hunger in a new, albeit unconventional way; which should not come as a surprise to him seeing as you've always been so clever. Asag will love that as he loves you. Easy peeeeazy! I could spin that no problemo." It killed Ray to kick D'mon's ass like this, but those sweet kisses would soon lube up the knife Ray had waiting for the former Soul Trader. "The past seven days can be explained as a logistic oversight by ahhhh, bureaucratic red tape blah blah blah."

They looked at each other and simultaneously said, "Red tape."

"Just promise me when you come back to Hell, you'll teach me some sales tricks." Ray embraced D'mon. The big demon was moderately grossed out. Old school Snake Oil salesmen used to call that the Tennessee Back Pat. One wasn't patting you out of consideration but rather looking for the sweet spot to stick the blade in.

D'mon nodded, "Ray, what happens to Asag if I don't come back?"

"Oh, he'll be fine, Lucifer has so many plans for him, I doubt it'll even matter much that you're gone. Don't worry about it, just have a good time here on Earth." Hound dogs for a thousand miles smelled Ray's bullshit yet becoming more a part of Earth now, D'mon did not.

"I hope so . . . he was by far the best director I've ever had. The way he leads by example with the whole team is motivating and inspiring; I'm just over the job and have been for years. It has nothing to do with him, please let him know that. There is a truth to your spin doctoring. Maybe by going on a human safari I will indeed be inspired and learn and awaken some sort of new hunger. Ha. Reverse vampires or some such."

"What?"

D'mon smiled and shook his head slightly.

"Nothing, Ray. Please tell him."

"You know I will."

"I don't want anything to happen to him, I'd feel terrible if I heard he was torn apart by 1000 ratigans at The Dark Lord's hand. if anything like that seems likely I'd go back in an instant, please let him know that."

"Happy to. Anything else I should tell him?" Ray noticed just exactly how large D'mon's penis was. He was staring. Jealous.

"What?"

"Nothing," Ray could not help but think that D'mon's penis was not monstrous, but it was indeed impressive and could be easily used to pistol whip a chubby Asian Cherub. Ray had a face only a demon mother could love and a penis that could rival only a runty gherkin. Motherfucker.

"Please… Tell him I care for him and respect him, and I appreciate his understanding." D'mon was anxious for the breeze to un-pause and the water to flow again. His human instincts were new and strange and powerful, trying to juggle his thoughts as a savvy

Demon and new born soul were unsettling. His perception was not at its best. Ray had slipped by the underhanded Demon side of D'mon and was welcomed by this new found earthly naiveté. It was this that helped endear Jessica to D'mon and lead him into the clutches of his manipulative co-worker as well. Even with human emotion clouding D'mon's savvy it would be no easy task to outwitting Ray Ma Ching, after all, he was to be a star in Hell.

SIX

When Ray Ma Ching finally did finish up his return at Transport, he half fluttered, half walked as fast as he could along the passageways to the grand office of the Director of Hell Admissions. He could feel the back and forth rumbling of the giant cock in which he worked. The insistent fucking Hell did to Earth every moment of every day was like the throbbing vibration of the engine of some huge ocean liner. Ray came in to see Asag lying on his fanciful red lace lined couch with a huge block of ice melting fast on his head. To see a Dragon's limbs all asunder was a sight to see as they didn't usually show their bellies, but it was obvious that the big dragon was agitated. He had a distinct scar aRo his right rack of ribs; an old war wound from Ambriel, a particularly ornery cherub in Mical's angelic platoon. That's what Dragons and other large creatures get for exposing their bellies in battle with smaller aggressive enemies. Doggy Park 101. Ray fluttered over more giant dead dinosaur fish lying on the office floor, some had smashed-in faces, all were blackened and practically turned to jerky.

"Boss?"

The red dragon muttered and rolled over a bit at the voice of

Ray Ma Ching. As Asag leaned forward he back-handed the lamp remaining on his desk shattering it against the wall.

"I broke everything else in this fuckin' office, why should the God damn lamp get to survive?" Ray's only response was the flatter of his tiny furry bat-like wings. Asag wiped his eyes with his wings trying to get his head clear.

"Well at least you returned, Id feared I'd be missing my number one and my number two." Fiery burp.

Ray brushed that stinging comment aside. He knew his big fat smarmy mouth wound betray him if he spoke his mind. His little Asian eyes widened to almost Caucasian dimensions, normally they were so squinty he could practically be blindfolded with dental floss. "I do as I'm told, Sir."

"So, you found him? Did you speak with him?" Asag coughed, almost singing Ray.

"Yes."

"That's good because while he's off gallivanting about we still have quotas to meet, that High Council meeting was not a joy, other Hells in other galaxies are beating our numbers this quarter. Plus, they wanted to know if I'd found a way to motivate him yet. Can you imagine all the eyes of representatives from all the worlds on me as I'm answering for a creature that slipped under our wall?" The Director's block of ice was nearly gone. Asag heaved a huge sigh. "Well? Give me some fucking good news."

"I can't Sir, there is none. D'mon has gone completely mad. He did nothing but rant and rave about Hell, the team, The Dark lord and, yes, even *you.*"

Asag sat up. His large tail whipped back and forth. "What did he say about me?"

"He said you were the worst boss he's ever had, and that your leadership is what took the thrill of his job away." Ray leaned his chubby face in close. "He said he even wished I was his Director." Yet the cherub's thoughts were more like *'number two employee my Charlie ass you big stupid red fuckin' turd.'* That was what was floating around in Ray's head. Ray was in heaven, metaphorically speaking, ironically too seeing this conversation was taking place in Hell.

"I see. Did he say anything else?" Asag was hurt and offended. Nostril fire shot out of the Fish Burner like smoke stacks from an Ozone polluting factory.

"He said that he hopes to see Asag the Fish Burner get torn apart by a 1000 ratigans at Lucifer's request." Ray watched as such a blasphemous statement sank in.

"That was his direct quote?" Suddenly the red dragon put his fist through his beautiful desk, a gift from someone in the Watergate Administration, splintering it into a thousand pieces.

"Sir, I found that comment to be sophomoric and lame. D'mon was just being hurtful, but he did say something I did take great vicarious offense to."

Asag just looked at him and motioned for him to spit it out.

The little demon looked around as if trying to safely avoid Fifth Avenue at Friday rush hour. He shook his little Asian head as if struggling with himself on whether or not he should share this insult with someone he respected and admired.

"D'mon called you . . ." Ray took a big sigh for dramatic effect, "obtuse, Sir!"

"Thank you for being honest with me, that can't be easy." Asag the Fish Burner could feel his dragon blood boil throughout his body. This Hellish Anti-Christ in waiting was totally and unequivocally butt hurt!

"I'm just here to help Sir."

The pink cabin surrounded them. Everywhere was pink. They had just gotten back from enjoying the wonderful fresh air and overhanging trees outside. Jessica's chest was heaving. She was just slightly winded. She had half jogged and half bounced back to her pink birdcage. Joy ran through her for the first time in a long while. She could not get rid of her smile. D'mon turned his neck, stretching it but not taking his new blue eyes off of Jessica for a second. He had just finished his run; sweat dripped off of him. Their gaze was locked on one another. D'mon too found himself with an uncontrollable smile. She glanced down observing a droplet of sweat trickle down D'mon's well defined dark body. It might as well have been a flood or an avalanche the way she followed it with her eyes. Her eyes widened. Once again locked with his. She bit her lip and sighed deeply. To D'mon, her freckles looked like brilliant constellations in the infinite night sky.

Emotions and ideas rocketed around both of their brains: *THINKING THE HELL THING IS SETTLED, AND* Jessica *BEING WARNED THAT D'MON WAS A BAD BOY...* Oh, Evelyn, thanks, but no thanks. These very important notions were of no importance at this moment in time when there was only one thing on both of their rejuvenated minds.

D'mon suddenly advanced towards her folding her into his arms. Her sweet breath mixed with his as their mouths came close, lips barely touching. Her pink lips pushed into his, kissing him was intoxicating. His hands pulled her close by the back of her neck. He was gentle and forceful all at the same time. She felt safe and protected in his arms. The back of her neck tingled and chilled as his fingers found their way down her spine. Sigh. Jessica lost herself in his neck, kissing it and running her tongue behind his ear. He pulled her back to kiss her yet again. There were no clothes to be ripped off only her pink towel between them. She pulled it away and practically threw it to the floor of the cabin. She pressed her flesh to his. Her breasts slid around his glistening abs. She reached for his body, her fingers searching the contours of his ribs and stomach. D'mon's hands too were searching around the naked writer's inviting body. He found her breasts with probing fingers. She could feel his manhood swelling against her body. She couldn't stand being denied what they both wanted. Jessica reached for his cock and gripped its shaft with the most straightforward of intentions. His blood was racing. His new human body was coursing with sensations he had exploited so lavishly against humans since the dawn of man and now was being devoured by them. Jessica's hand pulled slowly but firmly back and forth on D'mon's cock. She realized he was larger than the men she had experienced in her past. Derek couldn't hold D'mon's jock strap, metaphorically or physically. She could feel the beat of his heart by gripping his penis.

The animal feeling of having a soul were taking over D'mon. He turned her around, his hands now on her pale soft shoulders. Her hands refused to release their stubborn hold on his throbbing manhood. She stretched her fingers to maintain contact. His full lips began working their way down her back, his breath sending lightening down to her toes. His mouth inched lower and lower. As D'mon went lower inch by inch, Jessica reached for any part of him the she could. The former Soul Trader's lips continued on their journey lower and lower, his tongue trailing into the small of her back. His hands gripped her slender waist, bending her over, her belly meeting the cold tabletop. Her nipples felt the subtle cold sting of the varnished surface. Finally, her wanting hands were now too far from D'mon's cock; she grabbed the edge of the pink dinner table, her knuckles whitening, her fingers gripping.

His eyes opened to see the long deep arch in the red-haired writer's back as she leaned around the table. His hands slid from her hips down the sides of her legs. He could feel her quivering. His strong hands moved slowly upward, his mouth inching even further down. His teeth gently scraped her petite yet perfect ass, she could feel the nerves all the way in the back of her skull. He could feel her reaction, it thrilled him, biting into her. His teeth sent the exhilarating kind of pain one loves to endure deep into her soulless body. His heavy breath was like a beautiful fire washing over her backside. His tongue caressed her ass, sliding down between her awaiting cheeks. Her sighs told him to keep going.

His hot breath surged down between the back of her long legs. She was wet as Hell. He could feel her juices on his chin as he teased her asshole with his mouth and tongue. She tightened her body and then with one gasp of air surrendered to his intimate endeavors. She had not known anything that felt so good in all of her previous meek sex-capades. D'mon's tongue was gentle yet whip-like cracking against her ass and still further down to her soft folds. He could taste the milky sweetness from pleasuring her. His fingers now helping, ran deep into her. Jessica was pushing hard into D'mon's willing mouth, she could not contain herself in releasing her first orgasm. The electrifying feeling sizzled through every vein and every pore in her beautiful body. D'mon sighed with a hint of amusement. He was just getting started; enamored with Jessica and her trembling body.

He stood up behind her, his hands sliding arounnd her bottom and along the groove of her spine. His hard manhood pressed against her still twitching body.

"Do it. Please, put it in. Fuck me, D'mon."

His only reply was a bit of a growl. He was just as ready as she was. He wanted her in every way that was humanly or otherwise possible.

"Fuck me, D'mon, I want you."

D'mon rubbed himself along her moist folds lubing his shaft with her juices. He then pressed himself into her. Her wet vulva tightening around him. He overwhelmed her and yet he felt just right. Jessica was as scared as she was excited when she first saw his dark package. She had never had a penis that big inside her. *Derek who?* D'mon slowly moved back and forth using her wetness to paint his cock as a tantalizing means of getting as deep inside her as possible.

She looked back him her gaze was empowered and no longer naïve. She wanted him inside her and she wanted to cum more and more. In previous encounters if Jessica had come at all it was a bit of a miracle. Whether her lover was inadequate, or she was uptight, the fault would be shared, but now she was in new territory as she felt her second orgasm of the evening rush towards her. Jessica's body shook, her own private earthquake. If her clit was Tokyo, then a little tiny Godzilla just stomped the shit outta down town! She giggled.

"Holy fuck, oh my god. Keep fucking me!"

D'mon too chuckled thinking of the irony that this former Demon had just been referred to as God. Giggity! He kept thrusting. Her ass pushed back into his hips harder than ever. His fingers were leaving welcome red marks on each side of her waist. Faster and faster they moved as one, her pale beautiful behind banging against him over and over again. Jessica let out a loud singsong scream. Her third orgasm had arrived. Their rhythm was perfect. They kept going, writhing and breathing as one.

Jessica's body was taxed but willing ro push further into the depths of passion. Every groan and growl that came from D'mon lit up her senses like the Fourth of July. He almost sounded like some feral beast and she couldn't get enough of it or him for that matter.

He pulled the redheaded writer up from the pink table swinging her back into his arms. Their lips met again. She could taste her own wetness still on his lips. D'mon's hand reached under her picking her up and cupping her bottom easily. Her legs wrapped around him like the Burmese python she had seen earlier that day. Jessica's greedy hands again reached for D'mon's cock. She stroked it as they kissed. She inserted it once again deep inside her. She bounced and swiveled her body on his. His massive cock penetrating Jessica relentlessly until both of their bodies poured with sweat. Jessica was in Heaven (again, ironically, as her fourth time cumming happily destroyed her). He held her as they pressed up against the wall, her legs still wrapped tightly around the tall dark ex-demon. The lampshade sitting next to them barely stayed on the bulb it was attached to, no thanks to their bodies smashing against the pink walls of the pink cabin. They clawed and rooted around each other. Outside rain suddenly began to pour. Thunder cracked rocking the very foundation of the pink cabin. Or was it them? She and D'mon's breathing seemed to be in sync; their eyes locked. As Shakespeare would say, they hung by their bellies. The rain pounded against the windows as he pounded against her. The petite redhead looked at D'mon with anticipation. She wanted him to cum. She wanted him to share her joy, a joy that he was responsible for in every possible way. D'mon felt his body coming to a boil.

Jessica's inhibitions had been conquered. Now she felt alive and aware and could hear that specific growl and could feel the tremors deep with D'mon's chiseled physique. She knew D'mon was ready. D'mon sighed. Jessica swiftly slide herself off of D'mon's heaving body and slide his large cock into her mouth. Her lips wrapped around his shaft and he could feel the head of his dick pressing against the back of Jessica's throat. Her sweet breath filled his nostrils. His fingers snaked into her red locks of hair, bracing himself in front of her. Then his cock exploded into Jessica's mouth, filling her with his fluids and prowess. D'mon had never felt such emotions before and tears suddenly overtook the former Soul Trader. *'Human emotions are indeed powerful and unpredictable.'* he thought, no wonder humans acted in the ways that they did. Jessica's body was spent. Licking his demonic manhood, she gasped happily for air. Her tongue instigated the sensations that were devouring him, flicking and caressing his manhood. The sweaty naked writer had never experienced the acts of real lust before but was now well advised by a crash course in exquisite ecstasy. She finally understood what it was like to be swept away by a man and D'mon finally understood what it was to be a man with a soul.

The rain was still coming down like cats and dogs; the tiny sounds of water coming off of the gutters and the pinging of water against the windows was soothing to the two panting lovers. D'mon and Jessica both dropped to the carpet in joyful fatigue.

They giggled like playing children do. Nothing was wrong in the universe; it was only them, the only two people on Earth. Jessica arched her head back into her lover's chest. She again pressed her firm behind into his lap but now forming a spoon. She smirked and looked into his eyes.

"Oh, my fucking God. You da man, son. Ha. Fuck. Ho-lee shit. Not bad for a long-time listener, first time caller, wow." Jessica's fingers pretended to walk around D'mon's pecks like a little marching band. They were both marinating in the moment. Lightning flashed outside, which was unusual. Her tone changed suddenly. She let out a scream. In the quick glow of the otherwise dark night sky D'mon spun his head swiftly to try and see what his freckle faced lover was startled at.

"What, what is it?"

Oh my God, I must be seeing things. I could have sworn I just saw Evelyn at the window with Nakey wrapped around her."

The overflow of strange emotions roiled within D'mon, a hurricane of empathy, strength, anger, hurt and happiness. His body now contained a human soul that drove every fiber of his existence. A soul was not a mild thing, in fact it was one of the most powerful forms of energy throughout the Infinite. Angels, demons, Devils and Gods were all in the search to procure the infernal power source of life. D'mon was adapting to what was surging within him. His new emotions were becoming integrated into his thought processes and he could feel his logical and demonic sneakiness paying the price for his previous lack of conscience and morals. D'mon was perhaps the best Soul Trader that ever existed because he was nicer than other demons, so his connection to his prey was his strength. However, now that set of emotions was overwhelming him. The naked dark-skinned demon had been an expert in manipulation since before Unnk first created fire but now in this pink bird cage D'mon felt the tremendous power of the emotions he was a master of as opposed to just understanding them. He was adapting to this unprecedented download of energy.

He liked it and gave himself over to the process. There was now a human soul inside of him and D'mon like it. He liked it very much indeed.

The evidence of their pure carnal extravagance was all over the inside of the little pink cabin. Blankets and pillows were strewn about. In a mass of body parts at the center of the room a former Demon now in human flesh with a human soul pulsing inside of him was spooning with a wayward mixed-up soulless writer. He touched her red hair. He brought it to his nose and inhaled the fresh sex scented locks. So much coursed through D'mon; he was alive for the first time. They'd each celebrated a milestone for he was finally beyond the shackles of everyday ordinary sales and she had a winning manuscript set to make her a household name on bookshelves all over the world. She stretched and opened her eyes. She smiled brightly. He could not take his eyes off her.

"Hi." Jessica said as she looked over her shoulder. She nuzzled her back against his. She wondered how long he'd been awake. She stroked his dreadlocks, wrapping herself in their soft tendrils.

"Good morning." D'mon ran his fingers through her luscious red locks, then took hold tightly where it reached her scalp and pulled her head back.

"Red and white, you're my Tart."

"Ha. I like that," she purred. "Reminds me of Alice in Wonderland. Off with your head."

He released her hair and she kissed him with warm breath. She smelled of lavender body lotion that always reminded her of purple Pez candy from her youth. They held each other for a moment. One lost in dreams of the future, the other remembering what he had run away from. He pondered the details of the visit from the fat cherub. He hoped Asag was okay. That Ray hadn't lied to him about that. His emotions were indeed getting the best of him, but he was still a crafty demon nonetheless. D'mon had put his time in and was due an escape.

"I saw you cry last night," she was not teasing him. Her curiosity was pure, and he liked her concern.

"Your smell from down there burned my eyes," D'mon replied.

Jessica shoved herself away from D'mon in shock and looked back at him, "You're eeevil."

"Yup." He put both arms behind his head like a satisfied King.

"We both know my vagina smells like carnival rides and cotton candy, so don't be a jerk. You're trying to distract me from you feeling something last night." She adjusted her attitude from naïve to mischievous, so she could play his game. The writer somehow knew this whole soul thing was new for him as was her soullessness new to her. Jessica had stumbled onto a newfound strength within her empty chasm of existence.

"All I felt was nausea from rotten ovaries, you should get that checked."

"You are the worst, I'm done with you." She started to get up and he went for her, grabbed her around the waist and pulled her towards him.

"I don't know what I *feel* except this wasn't part of the plan. I didn't expect to feel anything."

"You . . . you girl," Jessica fired, "If you like me so much, how could you doom so many people like me, you asshole? You've got a soul in you now, chick's soul at that. I get that you should be an emotional diva right about now but, but . . ." she sighed in revulsion, "don't you feel any guilt you, you, asshole?"

"How can you swat a spider or step on an ant? Don't be melodramatic, they doomed themselves." D'mon broke eye contact not sure if what he was saying was correct or true. "Besides, the people whose calls I answer aren't typically your best goodwill ambassadors of the human race. A Middle Eastern man who will give anything to stop his daughter from becoming a lesbian or an ice-cream truck driver wanting to give his soul away just to see his favorite professional wrestler finally win the gold at WrestleMania, they have no idea what they are giving up for nothing. Some of these clowns make it really easy and they are contagious. Some soul selling is done by an entire sect or race or religious denomination. What perverted idiots ever thought female castration was a good idea? Ha!" D'mon looked back at Jessica feeling that that point brought him back into the white and out of the shades of grey, "Not even a blip on the radar, a human life is insignificant when compared to the eternal energy of a soul. Human life is but a single swift process in a long ass assembly line of Forever."

"I gave it away."

"You will be different. Your soul isn't in Hell, its right here." He placed her hand on his chest over his heart. "It'll be safe with me, and you will now live a long, full, fun, thrilling, exciting life and you know it." D'mon was honest for the first time ever with a human. It felt good whether she believed him or not. D'mon had his cake and was eating it too.

"My book is going to be a huge hit. It's going to touch lives. I'll set up a conference call with my agent in a bit. Don't forget the owner of this place wants you to meet with her."

"Do we have time left for one more round?"

"Now my smell is growing on you?" She flicked her fingers at his chin. It stung him, but he had to chuckle at her new born feistiness. He was smart, he knew he wasn't the only one going through changes.

He was a tiger looking at a gazelle.

"If I'm to be your Tart, there had better be."

"I think your burning bush is talking to me"

Jessica suddenly grabbed his powerful arm by the wrist and pulled it to her. She placed his large hand directly on her womanly folds. Her pussy was already wet. His fingers felt the small landing strip of red hair above her recently not so forbidden fruit. The tuft of hair prickled under his fingertips. He slid two fingers into her. Jessica arched back in pleasure, her body clenching around his hand. She hung off of the edge of their disheveled pink bed, now a disaster of pillows and sheets. D'mon's hand was the only thing keeping her from touching the ground. His fingers pushed in and out of her. Jessica's feet and toes pushed off of his legs, her ass bounced in the air between D'mon and the bed. He watched her, and she watched him right back. Her firm petite breasts bounced up and down as his hand worked.

"You do things I haven't enjoyed yet, oh, my God," Jessica gasped in the throes of the beginning of round two. "I'm not used to your surprises but keep them coming." Cumming! Her next noises were not words of any coherent nature, just groans and panting was all she could conjure. It wasn't long before her body exploded into even more ecstasy, "Fuuuuuuuuck!"

D'mon removed his hand from her wetness and pulled her legs over his shoulders as he leaned his knees onto the edge of the bed. Jessica looked scared and excited and ready. D'mon grabbed his already erect member using it to massage her tight pink lips and clit. Jessica gasped with joy, her eyes rolling back. The petite redhead sighed, her hands dug into the sheets, holding on for dear life. The pleasure was so immense. Jessica and D'mon's eyes were still locked on one another. He playfully slapped his large dick against her pussy; she let out an even louder moan. The head of his pulsing cock rubbed in and out of the folds but did not penetrate. He was teasing her. She loved that she could barely take it. He spit on his shaft for extra lubrication, mixing it with her sweet milky juices. He slid the head of his cock further down rubbing it around her asshole. He could feel her quiver and he was infatuated. She looked at him in fear combined with approval. He slowly, gently pushed his ebony erection into her rear hole. Jessica instantly exploded, orgasm number two was different, even more powerful than before. Anal sex was something she was alien to. She had been curious but always too shy or with Mr. Wrong. She could feel her muscles strain around his large member. It hurt wonderfully. D'mon thrust into her slowly at first and then picked up momentum as her body acclimated. He leaned down kissing her ribs and breasts then worked his way up to her pouting mouth.

Jessica's sweet breath was rejuvenating to D'mon. Their bodies shared sweat, their hands probing each other. They again locked eyes; her small hands gripped his powerfully muscled ass, helping his large cock travel in and out of hers. Her legs curled around his slim waist, her hands clawing at the sheets. His abs contracted as he moved in and out of her, sweat trickling through his definition like mice in a maze. His chest flexed as she tightened her body bracing herself for another explosive release.

"I'm cumming! Again! I'm cumming so hard, fuck!" Jessica couldn't contain herself. She was sure the entire nudist resort could hear her moans and screams but she couldn't possibly care less at the moment. She was still cumming, her body feeling like the wave of electricity would never stop.

"My ass! Fuck my ass! Your cock feels so good! My ass, holy fuck!" This was as vulgarly complimentary as she had ever been. Her words turned the former demon on and even surprised herself too, "You're cock feels so good inside my little ass, keep fucking me!"

Sweat was pouring off of D'mon's forehead dripping onto her, stinging her belly as he continued to drive his hips into the brilliant soulless writer. The sensations were growing in his cock as he listened to her scream and swear compliments and directions at him. "Faster. Slower. Oh my God. Yeah, yeah, yeah. Like that." His blood was boiling with passion and the sweet pain was washing over him.

"Fuck I'm cumming again." She was in a cloud of pleasure that she could barely comprehend. She wiggled, legs shaking. D'mon could not take it any more watching her in all her thrilling glory. The flood came crashing over the dark ex-Demon. The soul contained within him seemed to amplify everything he was feeling. It was like interdimensional Spanish Fly.

"Your body is so sexy. I can't take... I'm gonna..." D'mon could not string a sentence together as his body climaxed. He pulled his large cock out of her tight wet ass, aiming it at her small red landing strip. His body shook as semen shot around her heaving belly and breasts. The warm white cum splashed her. Her skin felt the syrupy sting. Jessica inhaled and exhaled heavily. Her body was relieved and satisfied and exhausted and ecstatic. The petite writer reached around her breasts rubbing D'mon's fluids into her soft white skin, smearing it around her nipples. The milky liquid dried quickly around her perky nipples and breasts, glazing her like a jelly donut... or a tart. D'mon collapsed on top of her, both of them happily winded.

SEVEN

velyn asked that D'mon meet her at her office located at the front of the resort. It had a magnificent view overlooking the Mount Baldy Mountains. Her office here at the Garden of Eden Nudist Resort was around from a large red Iron Gate adorned with a 'main entrance' sign. The small building was covered over with ivy and the looming branches of gigantic redwood trees. A clever doormat marked her office entrance delineating it from the adjacent laundry room and workout spa. It said, "A naked man fears no pickpocket."

"You don't belong here. You're not one of us," Evelyn sipped at her pink lemonade.

"A nudist, sure I am. Look I'm naked, aren't I? I'm sorry about the background check thing, I don't have a record yet, but I'll work on it. I don't want my darkness to disappoint. Stereotypes and all that . . ."

"Cut the crap, demon. I haven't lasted this long by being naïve and neither have you." The demon in human form relaxed, recognizing the situation and let his guard down. He thumbed through some of the naturist-themed items in the office. Then D'mon picked up a mug with the resort's logo on it.

"*Garden of Eden*, that sure is cute. All these years and you're still running around naked, even with your eyes open to modesty and shame. I don't mind though, I like perverts, it reminds me of home." He put his hands on the defined grooves of his pelvis, unveiling an unobstructed view of his impressive man-junk. Evelyn was not sheepish or coy in the least. She looked down, then up, one eyebrow raised, and lips pursed smugly.

"My place is wholesome, pure and without sin, you're the only pervert at my resort. An ungodly creature and as for my lifestyle I think you should know that I'm still talking to the snake, he knows you're here and he agrees that you don't belong."

"I don't belong in Hell either. Not anymore." He put the mug of pink lemonade down and rested his head on the seat in front of him. He thought he would give the sweet juice a try since he now had human taste buds, but it really wasn't his cup of tea, "I want to experience this place. Its pleasure and its pain intrigue me. I want to live among them. His chosen people, made in His image. I want to give it whirl."

"Let's go for a walk." The nudist gatekeeper and the ex-demon hiked up to a peak in the Mount Baldy Mountains. They stared at humanity from an elevated cliff far behind the resort. The entrance to this precipice was daunting and majestic. The two said nothing during their journey, Evelyn simply let the former Soul Trader soak it all in. Once they got there and stood for a minute or two she continued. "That is cute, you wanting to be among them, but it won't happen. For starters you don't deserve to be happy, demon. A wolf can't be friends with the sheep especially after a long ass history of slaughtering their families."

Demon looked off in the distance and saw the specks of life far below the mountain, cars and people like the crumbs of souls that would litter Hell. So many tortured and burning, eyes plucked out and spikes forced through their bodies from anus to mouth still gurgling with pain and innards but never to have relief. How many of these humans would suffer the same fate? How many at the hands of Demons even less talented than D'mon. He turned back to look at her. She looked into his eyes.

"It's D'mon, NOT demon."

"Funny, she called you Damon. Either way, I felt the ripples when you took someone's soul. Someone on my hallowed grounds. When I saw her in the morning and she was happy, I was conflicted." Evelyn staring into the ether. She reached back with both hands smacking her butt to encourage her circulation to step it up a notch, "She still had the breath of life, more so than in years but I knew demon, er, D'mon… that you'd robbed her of her essence. Another claim for Hell."

"I'm not taking it to Hell, lady. It rests within me… deep inside me. She will not be damned, and she will get her wish, plus I get to stick around here. Everyone wins."

Evelyn hadn't expected this. She pondered it, then brushed it off. "You speak with a forked tongue. I am aware you have seven days for her to change her mind. Those are the rules of fair soul exchange. Give it back to her."

D'mon stepped away from the old dumpy body of the All-Mother, mother of all human life. He stepped closer to the edge of the cliff. His bare feet pressed into the dirt at the edge of the precipice, broken bits disappearing into clouds of mist below. Evelyn took a bottle of perfume from her purse. "I'm too old to duel with creatures of the darkness, even during the day, so I thought I'd use this since my swashbuckling days are behind me now. This is pure one hundred percent Egyptian Palm Wine perfume. Back then they used it during the mummification ceremonies many lifetimes ago. Supposedly it gave the first "sweet breath" of the afterlife. It's far beyond extremely rare because its recipe has been lost and so only small amounts exist. Some people, and I use that term loosely, heretic bastards is more accurate, have *winged* it with Cedar Oil and Natron but the fucking hacks never get it right. Most of the stiff around is diluted down since nobody can figure it out. It is a lethal poison to an angel and if poured over the blade of a knife can wound or terminate one of those cocky fly boys lickety split. It is non-lethal to humans, but it can burn or poison anyone with an angel gene, and as you know there's no afterlife awaiting them. No stages... no moth, no cocoon, no butterfly, no life, no Heaven or Hell. There just *Is* or there *Is not*!"

"Yeah it can be tricky killing an Angel." D'mon had several run-ins throughout his travels. Barachiel had picked a fight with the former Soul Trader at a celestial rehab techniques convention three levels deep inside Limbo approximately five eons ago. Man, how time flies when you're immortal. It felt just like yesterday when that winged cunt tried to decapitate D'mon for checking out Mother Mary's ass as she stepped down from the pulpit. He was a douche, self-righteous and smug. The fucking angel might have succeeded if security wasn't first class. D'mon had peiced his heart with an onyx pitch fork but the crazy fucker just ripped it from his own bloody chest screaming "Let's dance, bitch!" Barachiel, what a nut job.

"It works on demons too."

"What the fuck? You're bluffing." D'mon looked quizzically at the bottle, calling her bluff. "I don't believe you. You are saying in that bottle is pure qeres?"

"The purest, but it's not only here, last night I also used it to dip the bullets in Henry's gun." D'mon saw a man in a suit step from the distance, no longer hidden by trees. Henry's way of saying hello was by spitting his chew into the grass and dirt. "You see Henry is not the father of humanity, he's just a mortal friend so he needed a little pixie dust to get the job done against the likes of Satan's minions. The demon put his arms in the air like an average crook and teetered on the edge of the cliff. Henry stood naked with his firearm locked and loaded, the black residue from his dip staining the rim of his slack jawed mouth. This felt like the Bible and Deliverance combo platter, D'mon was cosmically fucked.

"Alright, Listen, if you kill me, Jessica dies okay, she committed suicide that night. Her call to me was moments before she'd have died anyway, and no magic bullet could have saved her." He looked at them both in desperation. A devil pleading for understanding; that was fresh. "Now I'm not saying her soul was headed to fucking Hell for sure but think about it, she did kill a man moment before and based on what I had to clean up, I think it's a damn good chance her soul would get Hibatchied." He looked for reactions and saw nothing on Evelyn's poker face. She could and had dealt a winning hand or two. "If you shoot me, her flesh suit goes back to dead and the soul slips away to Hell knows where? Let me hold onto it for a while so that when it's released she gets a fair shot." At the word shot he looked at Henry's aim and reconsidered his words. "Rather she gets a fair chance... fair shake, fair fuckin chance!"

Evelyn motioned for Henry to wait on her command. She eyed Damien-ki Zakire Monteloflobe closely, having never seen a demon quite like this. If he was wearing a poker face as well she was impressed with it. As slick as fallen angels or born demons could be they did not stand a chance at out maneuvering, out bull-shiting the First Lady. Evelyn was suddenly curious, possibly even intrigued.

Just as Evelyn thought that she couldn't be more impressed by the sneaky ass demon's snake oil, D'mon impressed her even more. Tears began to fall from the tall dark ex-demon's blue eyes.

"Look, please. I didn't plan this, not really, anyway. I was miserable down there and this just kinda fell in my lap. I am so curious to see and feel what I have been taking from these sheep for so long. I fuckin' cried last night for fuck sakes. My first night as a man and I fuckin cry like a little God damned girl.

"Easy."

"Sorry, you know what I mean. Fuckin' Hell I'm crying now too. Fuck. I don't wanna die, lady.

"My name is Evelyn, not lady." *Demons can't cry,* she thought simply. This was weird. Maybe this asshole was telling the truth; stranger things have happened. She'd heard that God and the Devil still played golf once in awhile. But a long time had passed before they were actually cordial to each other, but time heals all wounds, yada, yada. They certainly were not best friends again, but they did enjoy each other's company on the cosmic back nine. If that wasn't a bit weird I don't know what else would qualify except a grown ass demon crying like a bitch. If D'mon was in fact telling the truth, then who knows how a soul would affect or infect a demon? Uncharted territory.

"You are beginning to care for her?" Evelyn grilled the tall, dark, naked new born.

"I just think she deserves a fair chance to be judged properly down the road, with more life experience." Evelyn thought about this. *Fuck*, she agreed. *Fuckity fuck.*

"Earlier I called you a wolf, well perhaps if the wolf looks like a sheep and talks like a sheep, over some time it'll begin to feel more like a sheep, only then can it begin any true atonement." She motioned for Henry to lower his weapon, but she kept her perfume at the ready.

"You take yourself away from here, demon. You're not welcome in my sanctuary."

"Very well, and my name still is D'mon by the way."

"If you've mislead me your name will be Stomped-nuts McRot-in-fire!

"I'll be gone by morning."

"Henry will give you a lift back to Jessica's cabin, say your goodbyes and try not to break her heart, D'mon. She has a great life ahead of her. I'm giving you safe passage out of here so don't risk it by trying anything with Henry, he's not my only guard." Henry smiled with that 'please try some shit you 'N-word' look on his fat uncle-dad face. The ex-Demon heard warning banjos in his head as he started to walk towards the truck. "One more thing; you might want to give your Boss a call, there's no sick days in Hell." She made a little giddy-up noise with her mouth, and then smiled.

After D'mon left, sitting in the back of Henry's truck, Evelyn put away the bottle and walked back along the trail to the office. Inside, she went to an adjacent room, where she kept the large tank holding Nakey. She lifted him out and let him slide on her desk. The skull pattern aRo its scales moved like a kaleidoscope if you watched the snake move for any length of time.

"Did you tell him to go back to Hell?" hissed the snake.

"I told him he doesn't belong here."

"That's not the same thing and you know it, you, m'dear are a trouble-maker. Hellarioussssss."

"Couldn't you tell him yourself?" Evelyn reached into a small green half-fridge in the corner of the office, pulling out a cold pitcher of pink lemonade to refill her empty glass.

"Ruin all the fun? Besides, I rather like where this is headed…" The serpent surveyed the heavy woman, watching as she bent over into the small icebox; her plump ass was a small abyss in which he would travel time and time again. The eyes of a serpent watching her every move as it moved closer… Evelyn filled her glass, took a swig, refilled it again setting it on top of the mini-fridge. The naked resort keeper bent back to return the pitcher, her head practically inside as the cold air touch her face, plump ass virtually up in the air.

Before Evelyn could shut the short green door, the snake was on her. Its fangs penetrating her ankle. Evelyn gasped, no time to let out a scream. Evelyn stayed frozen in her bent over pose half inside the fridge. The serpent removed his fangs from her flesh, slithering up her leg dragging the blood upward smearing the plasma around its scales. The snake navigated up her leg wrapping around her renaissance hips, then slid down between her portly butt cheeks and back up over her untrimmed nether region. The snake made its way up onto her belly, Evelyn moaned, feeling the moving scales pressing into her vagina, the coiling serpentine body pulling itself over her clit. The snake bit her yet again, this time in her side and then in less than a second her left breast where he remained suckling. The Burmese was a constrictor not a biter, but it could if it so desired. The All Mother held the fridge door bracing herself happily yet unwilling for her attacker to continue. Blood dripped down her curvaceous side and down in between the crack of her ass. Blood also came from her breast like rose-colored mother's milk. The snake could hear her heart and feel her in every way. The length of the snake had almost entirely passed around Evelyn's wet cunt. The tail seemed to have a mind of its own as it penetrated her body climbing deep into her most intimate secret garden. Evelyn's eyes were tearing up as D'mon's had minutes earlier, but she maintained. Blood started too dripping in a mixture of womanly juices and red. The old nudist stood petrified. The women shrieked as she held onto the small appliance; it shook under her weight until the pitcher of pink lemonade fell off of the shelf and onto the floor. By her feet pooled the concoction of womanly secretion, blood and pink lemonade; the foul ooze squished between her stubby toes. The snake released its fangs, retreating down on her in the same direction from which it had originally approached. As the snake left her she regained the ability to move again yet stayed motionless until Nakey hissed, granting her permission.

"Smile and dial team, it's the Earthly Hell Admissions power hour."

Ray Ma Ching sauntered past the offices of Representatives going through farm packs of humans who at a previous time in their life had uttered a willingness to give up their souls but for whatever reason never followed through on it. These souls were known as Ruby Reds or rubes. Some backing out before the seventh day and some not even making the initial agreement, memory of this was typically wiped from the humans themselves, but Hell kept tabs on every potential soul. Take for example Brooks Phillip Wilkerson; he was simply fed up with life, putting zero stock in the human race. Brooks wasn't exactly sure what he wanted out of life but knew he would have to bargain away his soul if anything substantial was to happen to the likes of him. Brooks, a window washer; wanted big things, to be adored by the humans that he thought useless . . . but what? His soul was ripe for the pickin's, a juicy apple of a soul just waiting to be plucked.

The rube's likeness was put on tarot cardesque office files. The soul energy that they held was well documented to prepare future demons in the hopes that their owners would be more susceptible and become a warm lead for Hell again at a later date. Each Rep would incite a brief incantation then light the card up on a black candle. It was pretty standard Hell magic only intended to work on the most susceptible of human minds, but in Hell beggars can't be choosers and with other Hells in other world's ranking higher in numbers, Ray was on a mission to motivate.

"Sell! Sell! Sell! Buy! Buy! Buy! Buy!" the chubby cherub shouted. Steve Baker had just sold his soul in exchange for being the proud new owner of Open Clam Gentlemen's Club in Huntsville, AL. The large spacecraft lining the highway wouldn't be the only things standing straight up in Rocket City on Steve's watch; his girls would be busy lil ASStronauts! Ronnie Johnson, too, sold her soul in this farm pack scramble; her ambition outreached her imagination. She wanted IT, she just didn't know what IT was until Zazzle Bee painted her a picture of her shitty, indecisive life. Since she had watched countless hours of Judge Judy in syndication whilst sitting on her lazy fat ass she was now a Justice of The Peace in Toronto. The number of dipshit humans was vast and ready to be moved and shaken.

Ray had a festive hat on and a horn in his tubby little mouth like it was New Year's Eve. He popped his head in on one of the Flout Nofs that had lost interest in the pile of cards on her desk and began sharpening his claws on her hind legs.

"Not enough leads Vanessa?"

Oh, I'm sorry Sir, I was just getting back to it."

The Flout Nof moaned in pain and pleasure; this was a confusing and common mixture in the Underworld. Screams came from the tall demoness, her 1950's skirt and beehive hairdo were quickly disheveled in the throes of Ray's pig hands tearing at her. The sensation devouring her was as if the cherub was going down on her. Her long legs were now bloody, and her fanged hissing pussy was now wet.

"See that you do. Dial into those souls. Give them what they desire most, and you'll be rewarded. If you're lucky I might even actually eat that cauldron pot you call a cunt." Ray spoke loud enough for the whole team to hear him. "Remember team, the person with the most appointments set for tomorrow, wins a free gift card for Rasputin's Aborted Baby Pizzaria. You know their slogan…" Vanessa says it with him. "Your loss is our sauce. Classy and delicious!"

"I get mine with a spilt troll sperm and bob a drink." Vanessa said as she took a card and began another rite in front of the black candle on her desk.

Ray continued his march of motivation up and down the halls watching as some team members marked off signs that appointments were set, and others showed signs of frustration. Buzzers went off when a rube was landed, telethon-style. Ray tooted his horn and smiled regardless, bleeding bullshit enthusiasm he hoped the team bought as genuine. He looked down at the stone floor, which was made from faces; soulless already purchased faces begging for their essence back. Better than tile flooring any day of the week Ray thought as he stepped on the faces.

"There's gold in the old." He hollered, knowing damn well it was easier to find a flea up a possessed polar bears asshole than convince someone that slipped away once already, but you never knew, every so often…

"I got six appointments set for tomorrow, Boss." Came the voice from one of the rep's offices. Upon Ray's inspection he saw that it was Cruz the Scarfel. "Can I stop now? I need to use the restroom and golly I had to go through over two hundred thousand cards just to set them." Cruz flashed a big grin, his fiery body licked at Ray. The fat cherub fluttered up into the air off the faces in the floor; avoiding Cruz' scorching exuberance. Ray was irritated as he patted his burnt elbow, blowing on it. He knew the scarfel meant well but it still fucking hurt. Ray had no threshold for pain he was a much better pitcher than catcher.

"Hey, pal, congratulations! You sure are a work horse, huh?" Ray gave him a big pat on the back. Fuck! Ray now had blisters all over his stubby fingers and palm, he fanned his hands in the Hellish ether. "We're so happy to have you on the team, keep it up and you may just beat 'ol Marge."

"Marge?"

"Yeah, she told us she could set way more appointments than you, told us that you don't belong on the team, and that scarfels are the bottom feeding vermin of Hell.

"Ahhh, that's sweet."

"It's not a compliment you exemplary scarfel, you. Sure, you can take a bathroom break if you want. You know what Marge does though? She uses a bucket. Take a look." Cruz leaned into the hall in the direction Ray pointed to see an office with nine buckets sitting in the hall. Each filled to the overflowing brim with chunky excrement attracting flies. Large flies buzzed around the buffet of shit. The deep chocolatey filled buckets spilled over with an oozing gelatinous mind of their own and had bubbles popping in it occasionally. The dark ooze was filled with corn, human fingers and other various tidbits floating therein.

Cruz looked at Ray. Ray looked at Cruz.

"I suddenly do not need to go, sir. I will be just fine. Maybe one bucket."

"We need to get Cruz a bucket over here!" fluffy white wings flapping.

With the balloons, confetti, and hustling in Hell's Admissions nobody noticed the streak of light hurling its way through Hell until it was beyond the front door and powering down into the lobby. Gabriel was a messenger Angel, 'God's Hero' who would bring mostly the good news. In place of a set of finely quaffed wings with tips dipped in solid gold like a standard Angel, he was gifted to be more of a glider, riding sunshine rays through even the dimmest and darkest depths of despair, none darker than Hell. As his radiating trail of light swept through the underworld it elicited various reactions from the demons that saw it. Some ran for cover and hid, others growled and hissed, and three very agitated Imps tossed spears in its direction. The power of his heavenly light disintegrated the spears on impact like matches tossed into a campfire. The trail led him to the lobby inside the giant cock forever fucking the Earth. Shirley and Tonya sat at the front desk in shock at the purity of the light and the form of a blond haired, white skinned gentleman in a cream-colored suit with red kerchief. The angel stepped out of the bright light that now dimmed around him. The two slutty demoness-secretaries looked at him letting their minds wonder, imagining what he would be like in the sack. Shirley thought he looked like a 'rusty trombone' kinda guy whereas Tonya was thinking he would be down with some ass to mouth play or perhaps he was a 'cum on her feet' sort. The angel looked like a walking fantasy to Shirley and Tonya; they could sense he would fulfill all of their *fantasy food groups*: 1 – Bring home the bacon, provide everything except when the woman was feeling all feminist. 2 - Let the women win the arguments especially when they are wrong. 3 - Treat them like princesses in public. 4 - Fuck them like whores behind closed doors… Yup, Gabe sure looked like a humdinger.

"Can we help you?" Shirley was imagining the blond messenger of God eating Black Forrest cake off her ass.

"May we help you?" Tonya chimed in pulling her whorish glasses down her little nose, eyeballing him. She was imagining the holy visitor snorting cocaine off of her large tits.

"Yes, I believe you can. I'm the Angel Gabriel, I'm here to relay a message from Heaven."

"From Heaven... wow..." The females swooned and began batting their eyes and playing with their hair. Going beyond innocent flirting, Tonya pulled her top down to reveal a pierced left nipple which she played with in a teasing manner as she eyed him up like he was a two-legged Happy Meal.

"Lust, yes, one of the seven deadly sins. This is why you belong here." Gabriel was disgusted, "and I do not." Thoughts of cumming on a she-devil's feet, humbug. Gabe would get off by listening to bird's chirp, choirs sing, pinkish orange sunsets, by being a goody fucking two shoes and celestial lap dog.

The door to the President's office opened quickly and President Duulexebub stood in his doorway hollering first at his front desk whores then pushing away the three-headed midget with face like a suckerfish that was orally servicing him. Its three sets of round eyes bulged as it plunged Duulexebub's cock. It was harder than you'd think (again, pardon the pun) for the demonic Pres to remove the midget's mouth that was still engulfing his sweaty hairy dick; a top of the line vacuum cleaner. "Jeeeeez you're a clingy little fucker, aren't cha! What was that? That God damned light?" Then noticing that the blinding light had left a man in the lobby he therefore adjusted his tone. "Gabriel, what a very welcome surprise. To what do we owe the honor?"

"I'm here to relay a message, may I meet with your Admissions department head please."

"Of course, I'll walk you over right now." He stoked his tiny mustache. The President was overly friendly, jolly even. He remembered how angels with sticklers for etiquette, one false move and this little fruitcake would turn into a fucking Terminator!

"No, please don't let me interrupt your adultery, please continue with your fornication. After all I'm not here to judge you." The President looked surprised, nodded a knowing nod. Beyond his door, past the pictures of his wife and family on his desk stood the three headed male Suckerfish trying its best to look inconspicuous. Licking its lips didn't help. "Nice tie. By the way, your zipper is down."

"Angels," The president laughed as he zipped up. "Can't hide anything from you guys." He adjusted his infernal cheap suit and began leading the way to Admissions. As they passed the whores gave a dirty look to the Suckerfish thing as he exited. The three-headed midget was mesmerized by the whore's large naked breasts and began to tug on his little weird deformed dinky. The Suckerfish snarled at the two secretaries, but they were too busy rubbing each other's nipples to care that they were being watched.

When Ray saw Gabriel coming his way he hollered for the team to continue and rushed to greet him. "Gabriel, you know I'm technically an Angel too." Bat wings fluttering extra fast whilst displacing the kind of smile the holy'iest of men would want to kick in.

"So were all Demons before the fall. I have a message to Admissions from Heaven."

"Right this way," Ray lead the angelic ambassador towards Asag's office with The President in tow. Once at the door, Ray motioned for him to check on Asag first in case he was busy. He ducked in quickly. The Fish Burner was preoccupied with providing a 'second' for a representative that was trying to convince a witch to sell her soul. Rarely did the team come into contact with someone with some knowledge of the afterlife and want to barter a higher quality deal, known as ringers or hookers throughout the industry. In these cases, a rep will call for a 'second' by the Director in which he was built up to be the deciding factor on acceptance to Hell. He would make it appear like Hell had a seat on a grand throne awaiting such a dark soul. Asag was a terrific second, obnoxiously and pompously confident to the point that it was contagious. Marketing and psychology would be a soul's downfall nine out of ten times. Thank God for Hollywood. It was all horseshit because in seven days their precious soul would end up as more morsels to dump on Lucifer's bulbous belly.

Ray watched Asag go through the motions by way of the enchanted mirror. They were in a special Wicca Herbs shop in suspended animation with the frustrated rep hoping Asag would save him his deal. Ultimately the ringer signed the papers and shook hands, no doubt looking forward to sharing this tale in a book or in a song as many of them did. I got one over on the devil my pretty! Like fucking shit, you did you dumb twat. Asag stepped through the large wall mirror with the rep following behind him. They then both regained their true form in the office. Gabriel watched as the rep changed from weathered old man to a cow sized dark green slimy blob with a million eyes all over it and the other old man split in two as a large red dragon grew from within. Asag kicked off the ripped and bloody human disguise as one might kick off muddy galoshes.

"That's how you out-witch a witch, son. She's locked in now so just follow up in a few days in a dream and keep her on the course. You got this, Conneaut Xy."

"Thank you, sir, that means a lot." respectfully replied Conneaut Xy.

The million-eyed blob-shaped demon stretched out large sticky moth wings from within its syrupy mass. The translucent wings then carried it out of the office. As the door opened a white light shone through.

"Who's out there, Ray? Is it God? Did God come? What does she look like?"

"It's not God." Said the white cherub, wings fluttering.

"Be straight with me Ray, I'm running out of fish." Asag farted a blast of flames.

"It's God's messenger, he wants to tell us something."

"Well, fucking fuck. They know. Does the President know?

"He's out there with him, I don't think he knows though."

Asag made some power faces in his enchanted mirror as if

preparing for a part in play or a film or some such. He lifted his eyebrows one at a time trying to look like the Rock or the Dos Equis guy if the Rock or the Dos Equis guy had been large red dragons. The Fish Burner then checked to see if he had anything stuck in his teeth. All clear, no unsightly body parts or spinach to be found amongst his giant fangs.

"Let's get this over with," Asag let out another big fiery cutting of the cheese.

Ray Ma Ching opened the door and once they were all settled Gabriel began. The angelic ambassador spoke with his eyes closed for the most part, this drove Ray, Duulexebub and Asag the Fish Burner all nuts. Gabriel quoted Scripture, he spoke in poems and was an irritatingly proper cunt. When he reaches for a feathered pen to sign a document he did so with his pinky raised. Ray cringed at the sight wanting to bite it off. They dredged through the various forms and celestial red-tape, non-disclosures, affidavits etc... Both the red dragon and the President watched as he did this with his eyes closed as if too good or snobby for sight. Heavenly witchcraft moved his quill and the parchments might as well have been doves fluttering in the air coming when called. Gay. Gabriel droned on about semantics and gave the politest ultimatums and threats that they had ever heard.

"You, Asag, The Fish Burner, I would speculate that you and your like will be thrilled to know, that Heaven is indeed unhappy with the way in which something was handled." the snobby angel announced. The President is perplexed. What was this holy cock-sucker spouting off about?

"Hell will be visited by two Archangels today," he paused with his God damn eyes still closed, "I entreat and encourage you lot to get a plan together immediately and fix what is so apparently broken. Judgement, I assure you, is coming."

President Duulexebub excused himself awkwardly. He rushed from the room to alert the heads of all departments, group texting on what looked like a piece of blacken lava rock. The President was trying to be useful for a change, his hurried departure left Gabriel alone with Asag the Fish Burner and Ray Ma Ching.

"You don't just get to prance into Hell," Ray closed the door and locked it. Gabriel smiled a blank emotionless smile.

"Certainly, I can. On the Lord God's accord, I can. You do know that I am even mentioned in The Christian Bible, several times no less?" Gabriel looked down at his neon white toga calmly dusting off a single piece of lint that dared land on him. *"While I was still in prayer, Gabriel, the man I had seen in the earlier vision, came to me in swift flight about the time of the evening sacrifice."* (Daniel 9:21 NIV version). His voice was extra pompous whilst he quoted the Good Book.

Asag began to get upset. The waters in his office bubbled up. A large prehistoric dinosaur fish rose its head up. It was pissed off although its hide was strong he wanted his master to be less angry. It eyed Gabriel. *You fucking douche,* the giant fish thought as its head burst into flames. Purple and green slime rolled out of the creature only to get turned to ash. The red Dragon stood straight up showing off his true stature, looking down his long snout at the Archangel Gabriel.

"Don't kill me." Gabe was instantly made aware of the reality check of all reality checks, "I'm the messenger, represented by the Earth's moon. I don't get physically involved in altercations. You would be literally killing the messenger! The archangels are still coming no matter what."

Asag cringed at the way Gabriel said the word 'what' like it had five 'H's in front of it. This and this alone was enough to help the Fish Burner decide Gabriel's fate. Asag's wings stretched to their full expanse and the angel found himself clothed in shadow.

"Lovely, bring them on. I'm not killing you because you're the messenger. I'm not even killing you because you're a shit-stirring little pussy. Hell, I'm not even killing you at all. My fish however . . ."

A giant Ctenurella rose out of the water and chomped down

onto Gabriel's head all the way down to the douche angel's shoulders. It had a long whipping tail and large glowing prehistoric eyes framed by a robust lower jaw and giant teeth. Gabriel shot flashes of light in different directions from holes in his celestial flesh. However, he tried to fight, but his skills were fishy at best! The grimacing Ctenurella was equipped with large hook-shaped sex organs known affectionately as claspers (Oh, God or Science or whatever you call yourself you are a sick little monkey). The sharp serrated sperm delivery system dug deep and painfully into Gabriel piercing his glowing broken body. The Heavenly ambassador exploded into a splatter of light and prehistoric fish eggs. A messenger Angel was never meant to be a fighter especially not of dino-demons from Hell.

Ray, the Assistant Director, President Duulexebub and Asag the head of Admissions just stood there silently for a moment in the large Hellish office letting what just happened to an angel from the fucking Goddamn Bible just sink in a bit.

"You can't do that, he's in the Bible!" Ray freaked out, the little Asian cherub smelled of sulfur and fear marinated in a squirt of urine.

"Yeah well, so is Goliath and how'd that turn out for him?" Asag elbowed Duulexebub in the ribs.

Asag gripped his massive dinosaur-fish-thing, still chomping on the cream-suited Angel remnants, and put him back in the large tank, now with cooled down water. It was a good thing that Asag was huge because the Ctenurella was no small beast; it yelped under the grip of the Fish Burner and again as it splashed back into its tank. Ray was beside himself, panicking while Duulexebub had thoughts of a foursome with Shirley, Tonya and the Ctenurella.

Asag began to prepare himself for the big meeting with even more important Angels than the one that they had just allowed to get prehistoric-fish-raped to death.

"We have to get our defenses ready because I'm sure it won't take them too long to…"

There was no explosion, no white light nor harps playing melodic cherub songs, they were just suddenly there. It was blink of an eye and miss it 'I dream of Genie' type shit. Two people stood quietly before them that were not there the wink of a nose ago. The two new-comers stood side by side looking at each other then brought their gaze to Ray, Duulexebub and Asag. The two men were not ominous in the least, which made them really fucking ominous as far as the three demons were concerned. Both creatures wore red gowns with sashes. The first looked like the actor George Clooney in the 90's, the second looked like the TV wrestler Ric Flair in the 80's.

"I am Archangel zadZiel. I represent the Mercy of God. I am His righteous hand encouraging those before me to know that God cares for those who confess and are repentant of their sins and thus know that God will be merciful in return." when the first man spoke the voice did not seem to come from his mouth but from all around.

"Okay…" Ray murmured.

The two men stood emotionless and motionless in the midst of Hell.

"We await your solution."

"A solution for what? There's no problem here guys," Duulexebub blathered like a back peddling used car salesman.

"Speak falsely once more. One single word and it shall be your last, Demon." again zadZiel's voice seemed to come from nowhere and everywhere. "Please do not provoke me into showing you the other side of God's righteous hand."

The second creature remained silent. Asag grumbled. Ray assessed the situation frantically thinking of any way possible to save his Asian cherub skin.

"A solution, now," zadZiel commanded.

"Well you see there are different channels thru which we delegate out courses of action. We also value our Earthly R and D team and encourage them to think outside of the box. This might seem a tad avant garde but I assure . . ." Asag was interrupted by the second creature.

"I am Archangel Mical. I am your Lord and Savior's mightiest. I am the leader of all angels and owner of the sun." The moment he said the name Mical the three demons knew exactly who he was and his accolades, but none wanted to interrupt. His voice, like his partner's, was all encompassing. They knew him very well seeing as he was the guy that shit canned their boss Lucifer out of Heaven in the Great Divorce. They did not however know the part about him owning the fuckin' sun. Was that new?

"I have no need for formalities, problems, excuses or rapport, only solutions," Mical continued.

"Michael, I would like to . . ." Asag was trying to accommodate the Archangel but wasn't making much headway.

"Mical."

"My bad, Mical." *Well lah dee dah*, Asag over-pronounced the name. Mical had earned the right to flaunt how fancy his name was in Angelic script. "May we have some time to get our ducks in a row?" He heaved a big sigh, "You got here so fast we haven't had a second, literally, to even prepare you a proper welcome let alone a solution." Duulexebub stuck his head outside the office and whistled. Not a minute later several short, pudgy red penguins with long devil horns appeared with a solid gold carpet to greet the angels on their first steps in the Underworld. zadZiel looked at Mical then they both looked at the golden roll but were not impressed. Mical waved his hand nonchalantly and suddenly without a puff of smoke or holy song the golden carpet was no more. The two Archangels took several steps towards Asag leaving pure gold footprints behind them.

"Damn!" Ray said out loud by accident, his mental filter on the fritz for just a moment. Mical was so powerful that it was even told in the Koran that his tears birthed all cherubim. Ray Ma Ching was a cherub. *Dad?* Ray thought to himself. *Perhaps your shit birthed Demons.*

"You, you will order a meeting with all department heads, Mr. President." delegated Mical. Duulexebub, shat slightly in his cheap suit. "Nice tie." Duulexebub, Ray and Asag all thought that this must be good news; another flood, plague, the God damned Rapture? When Archangels get involved in private meetings inside a giant cock located in fucking Hell of all places, well that's a big deal but not necessarily a war. What exactly was this Holy Shit?

"And you, Asag, you will warn all of the denizens of Hell. Is that clear?" The two Archangels looked at each other silently for another moment. It was creepy! Were those two fuckers communicating telepathically or were they just being shitheads playing cosmic mind games? "We know your abomination's name is Damien-ki Zakire Monteloflobe, born of a distant Hell. He was the first to take the risk, he'll be the first to pay the price. We need to send a message to any beings, be they winged or cloven hoofed that consider breaking the boundary line in the space between the worlds!"

"When we announce the breach for the first time before we have contained it." Asag argued, "It will cause more chaos than we can manufacture. All will be in shock! Pandemonium will run rampant; and I hate that bitch." Pandemonium was going to have a field day with this scandal, that tall cunt lived for this shit as an Infernal C.O.O. with the highest of pay grades. "What will Lucifer say?"

"Seven days is the duration of our warrantee!" Ray jumped in. His outburst was brilliantly timed if he did say so himself.

"You still have some time within the seven-day grace period to bring him back. That is our only leniency." zadZiel announced. "We'll grant you that this is some new sales tactic you have tried allowing him on Earth this long. But mark my words demons. Past the seventh day and it is War. We will collect your demon iby Godly force if you cannot do so by your own conventional means. Don't wait for us and do not make us wait. This is the Word of God."

Mical looked at Asag, it was hard to tell if the Archangel was going to agree with zadZiel or say 'fuck it' and smite them all right here and now. Then Mical's voice filled the room. "The Morning Star and I have… history. Lucifer knows the sincerity of my words and actions. Besides, he already knows, and he very much wishes to speak with you, Asag." The big red Dragon vomited in his mouth.

EIGHT

Jessica Ro drove her black MX-5 Miata from high in the twisty turny Mount Baldy mountains down through the desolate nothingness of the Inland Empire. She had the ragtop down enjoying the wind as it ravaged her red hair on to the way to the southernmost part of California. She'd packed up a few things from the little pink cabin and was off to celebrate the success of her first sold novel. Even with an assist from her soul-trading lover who sat next to her in the passenger seat. He appeared to be an African American man with dreadlocks just as every white man with a ponytail looks like Steven Segal or the comic book guy from The Simpsons. Her yellow flower-patterned summer dress had a mind of its own blowing around in the cockpit of the breezy convertible. Jessica had to push the front of her cotton dress down every so often tucking it under her leg to keep it from flying into her face as she drove. D'mon looked at her with a playfully sinister smile which she happily returned while unveiling the fact that she was not wearing any panties. She bit her lip suggestively.

"You'll love my friends," Jessica said. "David and Chrissy are the best. I was at their wedding. They got married on Black's

Beach, that's a popular California nudist beach. I remember how…" D'mon gazed out the window seeing nothing but freeway and let her keep talking. He'd discovered that's what human females love to do more than just about anything else. The California air was intoxicating. He soaked up the world with fresh human eyes. He'd encouraged her to show him more of the Golden State than just the resort, telling her how they should celebrate her impending success.

Fame would be a brand-new thing for her to experience just as everything in California and the world was new to the ex-demon. Her publisher offered her an unfathomable six-figure advance on her debut novel as well as a Ro country signing tour. Life was good. In two hours from the time they packed up they were heading southbound on the 15, with D'mon putting the threat of qeres tipped bullets far behind him. They stopped off for gas, enjoyed a couple of frosty fresh slushies and hotdogs and then were back on the road. Hotdogs seemed oddly funny and phallic to D'mon and very messy as well. He was getting mustard and ketchup all over his hands but 'When in Rome' as they say. All the while they listened and laughed along with talk radio and standup comedy albums. George Carlin, you, silly genius bastard, Robin Williams, you tormented soul. Time flew pleasantly by for the two lovers and when they arrived at the quaint little home it was nearing nightfall. Her friends had waited to greet them. The two middle-aged white people came rushing out like a couple of Springer spaniels.

David was a good person. He was a simple man who loved nudism, tinkering on cars, his wife and Disneyland, not necessarily in that exact order. Chrissy was also a genuine good person. She loved her fashion design business as well as nudist activism in areas like topless freedom for girls and the rights of women and body acceptance in general. She was a guest speaker at colleges on the subject and had been trying to have a baby in recent years. Together they couldn't have been more in love. Their place was also the home of Loxie and Zoot, two friendly tuxedo cats. The felines were friendly to most, skittish at worst and had never hissed at anyone until they met D'mon. His demon genes apparently setting off instinctual alarms. The couple enjoyed each other's company and D'mon could see how happy Jessica was in their company. They settled into the guest bedroom and after a few drinks they separated for the night. All was still in the San Diego home. The waves of the Pacific crashed in the distance spreading a gentle saltiness into the air.

In the morning they all went to Black's Beach. They parked and hiked far down the cliffs to reach the beach. The four of them played volleyball with other nudists, and enjoyed watermelon served by some friendly nudist greeters.

"Nudists love greeting new people and hearing what brings them to nudism, just like Christians love hearing how people find their way to God." Jessica explained. D'mon cringed ever so slightly at the example.

"Maybe the Sun is ultimately the nudist's god?" the ex-Soul Trader fired back playfully.

"Maybe, dick."

The Memphis style BBQ stained the air with deliciousness. As a newborn human, D'mon quickly grew to understand why so many people thought with their stomachs. This shit was awesome; messy, but awesome. The BBQ sauce got in between his fingers and he could feel it sticking around the corners of his mouth. Jessica helped wipe the hickory goodness from D'mon's face with wet naps laughing at how he could seem so mysterious and sexy one minute and then act just like a silly little kid the next.

Everyone was discussing the World Naked Bike Ride event that was happening in Los Angeles the next day. Everyone was excited but D'mon felt as though riding a bicycle with no clothes on sounded a tad uncomfortable to the point of it being masochistic. *Whatcha doin' tomorrow, Fred? Ohhh, I'm gonna wedge this bike seat into my ass while I peddle my balls off!* D'mon chuckled at the thoughts inside his head. He pictured a fat, middle-aged Lothario leering at the fine and fancy girl butts around him as he wore a hole in his scrotum on the seat of his racing bike.

"David and Chrissy offered to lend us extra bicycles if you wanna do it?" Jessica motioned as if she was on a bike speeding down a curvy hill.

Making new friends sounded like a step in the right direction to D'mon. He couldn't rationally put his finger on why, but he was sure it had to do with his needy new human emotions. This lovely married couple seemed like a good place to start. They were already friends with his lover and they just seemed nice. They had funny things to say which amused him. Chrissy would joke with David about how it was cold and 'nippley' outside as she flicked her own breast. David would return fire sheepishly by doing the same to himself. They spoke articulately of politics and art and current events in a manner D'mon found useful, educational and entertaining. They were indeed 'friend material'. He saw the way David looked at Chrissy, enjoying her presence, her short blond hair and her big bright toothpaste commercial smile. He saw the way Chrissy giggled at David's sense of humor and always found a reason to touch him. Over and above that, they were sweet and encouraging to Jessica. She deserved that he thought.

Nudist families of all shapes and sizes were outside enjoying the day. They were getting in the ocean water, laughing, splashing and lying out like fattened sea lions. For the ex-demon this day was especially wonderful. He soaked up different things about people on a ground level that he had never noticed in all of his time spent as a Soul Trader. Emotions and relationships were now more than something he observed, he was now living it, laughing and interacting. He noticed how he enjoyed ketchup and fart jokes and was put off by arm pit hair and people that wore mustaches without beards. Idiosyncrasies formed in D'mon's brain forged with new heightened senses. Some things were completely trivial, and he knew it, like Peter Walsh's generous amount of arm pit hair, although his skills with BBQ pork way more than made up for it. There were a great many other things he realized were valid and important like views on taxes and animal rights and deficit spending. He enjoyed listening to Jessica and Chrissy talk about some of the animal kill shelters that Chrissy had helped adopt animals from and the kind people that took the creatures in. The human condition was so very much more than vain wishes. D'mon had spent a millennium negotiating with mostly the dregs of humanity and this had most definitely given the ex-demon a jaundiced view of the human race. As it turned out, humans had selflessness and kindness within them that he had never even been aware in all his centuries of nefarious negotiations. But now, Thanks to his redheaded writer, D'mon was witnessing first hand.

D'mon watched with intense interest as people went paragliding and surfing and he wanted to try it all. Seeing extreme sports in the nude was fascinating to him. Would it be like this every day as a human, discovering ketchup fart jokes and paragliding and surfing and who knew what else? Oh, the wonder of it all! Jessica saw the way D'mon stared at the paragliders like an enamored child.

"Would you like to try that? I know Steven; he is one of the instructors."

"Ummmmmm. Yes, yes, I would!" replied the ex-demon.

Not long after some introductions and a crash course on body postures and procedures Damien-ki Zakire Monteloflobe was soaring above the waves of Blacks Beach, a giant bright-colored bird dancing with the wind. His hands gripped the harnessing straps. He could feel the tension of the ropes leading to the bright yellow and green-striped chute above him. He looked around lost in the breathtaking view that surrounded him. Mountains rose up into the sky far to one side, endless ocean, blue and serene on the other. Below his feet stretched beautiful white sand and the Heavens gleamed turquoise above. *Holy shit, was this what it felt like to be an angel?* D'mon thought to himself. His safety goggles stained the sky bright yellow, rushing wind pressed against his face. *No wonder those fuckin' fuckers loved to fly.* What seemed like a fun-filled eternity went by swiftly. The ex-demon smiled constantly as he flew thru the cerulean fastness of the endless sky. He could see Jessica waving at him far below and he realized that even way up here he was not alone. It was a good feeling. Fuck no, it was a *great* feeling!

The wind was choppy and wanted D'mon back on earth. The parachute was descending as the crystal waves approached. It felt to D'mon as though this was his own private fall from grace. Jessica gripped her dear friend's shoulders hard as she watched her lover heading for the water at a rapid rate.

"Ouch, you fucker, ha let me go! He will be okay, he's big and strong." Chrissy barked at Jessica, not worried at the situation. That's why you paraglide over water because it is way more forgiving then concrete or any other type of solid ground. D'mon hit the water and his chute imploded into a giant sash of bright yellow and green rip-stop Nylon. The water shot up around D'mon like a fountain. As the waves crashed, D'mon came to the surface, whipping his dreadlocks from side to side. The ex-demon looked more like some powerful African god. Jessica's heart skipped a beat. "I told you, dick, he would be okay."

As D'mon waded out of the ocean dripping Jessica barreled into him with an endearing hug.

"You scared me, ha-ha, you dickhead. I hope that was fun, D'mon. Hahaha you looked pretty hot up there." Jessica was happy, "Flying high in the sky, my sexy guy, my very own angel." She gave D'mon a playful conspiratorial wink.

"Shut up. Very funny, *dickhead.*" D'mon had to laugh. Jessica's ironic humor and devilish choice of words was not wasted on him but further proved to him that she was special and worth every risk he was taking. "That was super fun, but the landing killed my balls though, fuck."

They both laughed a bit. She looked around both ways as if making sure it was safe to Ro the street.

"Well, if you play your cards right, pal, I will kiss them all better." This was not boring soap opera shit to either Jessica or D'mon, they were both discovering real, true happiness. Her arms were wrapped tightly around him, his arms reciprocating. He didn't want this moment to end. Not ever.

D'mon wanted to say the words… He felt the words on the tip of his tongue. They were powerful words, not be used frivolously. Whether it was God or the Devil that had turned *love* into a necessary evil was unclear, but its allure was much sought after and in high demand by both sides of the cosmic ether.

Before the moment got too serious and L-bombs could be dropped, D'mon and Jessica found themselves being hugged by David and Chrissy. The other couple was playful and interrupted as much out play as they did out of caring. As far as the redheaded writer was concerned, they were the greatest friends ever.

"Sorry, couldn't help it kids!" Chrissy stood strong and sweet, her arms stretching around the others. Chrissy being Chrissy grabbed Jessica's behind. "You've got a great ass by the way, Marcy."

"Chrissy!" Jessica swatted away her friend's hands, laughing and blushing her freckles into oblivion. "Marcy? I hate that name. Jessica, if you please young lady." They both laughed and hugged some more.

David smiled and D'mon couldn't help but noticed people had ridiculous ways of bonding and he enjoyed every second of it. *Maybe David and Chrissy were the greatest friends ever,* he thought.

"Upsie daisy." Chrissy stole one last *honk-honk* from Jessica's petite white ass before letting go.

"You're crazy," Jessica choked the words out while giggling.

"Uh, I'm pregnant, bitches!"

"Shut the front door!" Jessica uttered one of those very high-pitched girly screams that pissed off dogs for miles around.

"If she did shut the front door we wouldn't have this kick ass news to share." injected David dryly with a smirk.

"Touché!" Jessica leaned in to examine Chrissy's perfectly tanned stomach.

"It has been four weeks today! I was waiting to tell you and it was kaaaaa-illing me. I wanted to tell you so bad last night, but I didn't wanna jinx it until I hit the four-week mark." Chrissy was more or less hopping up and down as she spoke. D'mon thought that her quaint superstition was kind of adorable.

Happiness in the sun. Could life be any better? Life certainly was a curious sort of theatre and Damien-ki Zakire Monteloflobe felt like had just purchased front row seats.

"Fucking fuck, fuck shit, shit, fuck, FUCK," Asag, the Fish Burner sounded like he had Tourette's syndrome marinated in cocaine as he made his way through the wormholes and passages toward the meeting place. He felt like one of the tiniest fish in his massive holding tank, one that would hide from the larger fish hoping to survive another day. The red dragon trekked thru the twisting passageways, his wings scraping the cavernous walls. Being called to speak with Lucifer himself one-on-one was not something he looked forward to. As any counsel with this powerful, legendary entity who was known by many names: Beelzebub, Old Scratch, Satan, The Devil, or even The Big Boss, could readily end with disastrous results for anyone, even the Demon of the highest order. Asag was the one knighted above all others with the title of Director of Hell Admissions or as a human might call him, The Antichrist. When you are at the very top there's no place to go but down and down was a very long way from where he presently stood. Asag contorted and turned his long red dragon body to bend around the curves of the tunnel making his way through. Lucifer did not appear in real life the way he was shown in media and advertising, where his image was supported by and refined by some of the best intentioned Dark Artists and Soul Traders. His image to the staff as well as that on Earth was never allowed to show him as less powerful than a giant hoofed and horned muscle-bound Hellion oftentimes holding a triumphant pitchfork at his side, his pointed tail flicking about. Often, He was shown in the image of a red suited gentleman with a goatee and fire behind his eyes looking to play chess with God for someone's soul. Both of those images were well manufactured by the infernal machine of the Promotional Department but at the top of the food chain, Asag and others on the High Council were privy to the truth of his existence. That truth was not pretty, but then Hell often wasn't.

The Fish Burner reached the end of the lava tube. In his youth he'd been given an ant farm from the hive of angels of the Red Dragon order that raised him. Ants were special because they had to be imported from below and he spent many cherished hours watching them dig about in the clouds making their tunnels and creating a life for themselves. It was a fun memory from his childhood. Asag kept them deep underground in the meadows of the thickest billows so that the heat surges from the sun wouldn't kill them. He loved them until one day they began slowly dying, not from any torture but just the passage of life, only a few passed away, but Asag saw that the others would soon go following their leaders into that place where ants go when they run out of life force at last, he felt bad for them being confined to such a prison, so he released them, freed them to have endless possibilities. He recalled ripping the lid off and encouraging them to go. Almost immediately water spiders swooped down and caught them all in their webbing. Asag tried to save them but it was futile, and all of his precious pets were lost to the wild Heavens. Asag learned that day that freedom is not always a good thing and sometimes the rules and boundaries are in place to protect us from what is worse that could be waiting beyond the walls of what we know. He felt like one of his ants in the ant farm as he continued towards the opening at the end of the tunnel, the distance beckoning and glowing with its lava red light.

The Fish Burner stepped out of the opening in the rock and stood before a grand swamp of bubbling, gelatinous magma goo. It snapped and popped with frothy suds rising from its murky depths. This was the core of all things on planet Earth. The goo was eternal and stretched so far it was lost to the sight long before edges of the cave walls. These cave walls were decorated with souls being fucked against their will. The walls moved with the pain and suffering of every facet of molestation. Faceless and or deformed dead people were enjoyed and tortured all over at their own expense. Their skin was the color and texture of the rock, they were the rock, the foundations of Hell itself. In the center of it all, bathing waist deep in the lava and soulful agony was a creature of titanic proportions. Asag squinted his eyes adjusting to the oddly lit Lake of Fire before him. He realized as his eyes focused that the massive being was built entirely of misery. Every manner of rape, surgery, and torment was going on constantly from within its skin, these twisted tortured creatures pushed fruitlessly against the tough hide that enveloped them. They fought desperately trying to get out which fueled the huge being's enjoyment. Those practices that comprised this large creature were created and enjoyed on Earth and various other areas of the ocean of infinite worlds. Asag witnessed a luxury resort of pure pain the likes of which even made the Red Dragon squeamish. Suddenly he realized how uncomfortable he had become in the presence of pure unadulter- ated Evil. The wormy tunnel that lead Asag to this vile place tight- ened and closed behind him with an unpleasant crunchy squishy sound, a stony sphincter of red hot rock. The Fish Burner was now completely stranded in Morning Star's favorite communication portal. It was quieter here and Lucifer would take audience here and only here amongst the most damned of the damned. Asag sat on a rock at the edge of the bubbling goo and waited, watching the huge monster bathe. Lucifer knew he was there and would communicate in his own good time.

The huge King of all demons let fly a titanic fart. Indeed, an epic fart! One of legendary proportions in both the smell of rotten, decaying flesh. The incredible stench hung in the stuffy hot air as the shit-snot goo was tossed from ass towards the roof of the cavern of damned souls. Even Asgag's bloodshot dragon eyes watered at the acrid aroma of it. The giant rape covered beast palmed a handful of the excrement that caked the top of the lava, brought it to its nose for a pleasurable whiff before flinging it away. The rapey, corny turd landed with a splat bukakeing the tormented souls that comprised the walls. The Morning Star's aim was a perfect as a big-league pitcher's. The disgusting mess flopped against the wall directly over where the mouth of the now tightly puckered sphincter tunnel. The excrement puddle rippled and belched. Asag stared at it, giving his Dark Lord his full attention.

"You lost one of my favorite workers, Fish Burner."

"Yes, he is on the surface, but you know that already."

"He does not wish to return, but he will if you visit him. Damien-ki Zakire Monteloflobe, the demon known as D'mon respects you and your leadership. He will return if you reach out to him. Will you reach out to him?" Lucifer was not asking, he was commanding.

"Yes of course m'lord."

"Good." The substance created out of pure rape and torture burped and farted all around the Dark Prince. "I was amused at D'mon's clever use of seven-day lock. Hoist by my own petard!" Lucifer threw back his horned head a laughed heartily. The sound was what a few hydrogen bombs would sound like if the were detonated in a bathroom. "Those seven days are his treasure and Hell's semantic cock up. The duration means nothing to me. If I want a soul or anything else I will take it... Right or wrong, I don't give God's green shit. Everyone is tippy toeing around the seven days unsure and scared. 'Unprecedented' is a word I've been hearing. Ha. Everything is unprecedented. Any illusion otherwise is just celestial ego. Rules were and are meant to broken, but only when I fucking say so. Will D'mon go to Limbo? What will become of Jessica Ro' surrogate soul? All that power awarded to a Demon? He must really be quite something. Now that's how you stir shit up in the universe! I'm enjoying watching the tube as long as I have the remote in my hand but as soon as I have to get up to change the channel… well that just won't do my son. And furthermore, there will be NO QUESTIONS unless I have ALL OF THE ANSWERS FIRST! God forbid something new should create havoc in this well-ordered cosmos. Hmmm. Fuck that! I fucking forbid it, Asag! I fucking forbid it! I'm the only one that has any balls in this universe. D'mon is no Lucifer. That grunt is no beautiful Morning Star. Find your nigger boy, and find him YESTERDAY, Asag, MY Fish Burner, before you both Fall from My Grace, and that, sonny boy is a long fucking way down! If you thought the drop from up there was steep just wait until you see *how low, you can go.*

A stream of hot reeking urine trickled down Asag's scaly leg, the greenish piss hissed and then disintegrated as it touched the sodomizing floor beneath his talons. Lucifer took the Director of Admissions, or as he preferred to think of him, the Antichrist in Waiting soiling himself as a sign of Asog's keen understanding of the situation he found himself in.

"Then shortly all will be well, no harm no foul. I prefer to keep things gentlemanly and pleasant here in Hell. I'm not a monster!" The huge cavern rang with the bomb blast of laughter that erupted from Lucifer's throat. "Let's celebrate the occasion with a bit of fine dining. Whadaya say?" Two golden plates glided on top of the shit-lake of goo. They reached the shore and beached there in front of the red dragon. Asag removed the golden lid from the first plate and saw a pile of small human fleshy limbs. Under the second lid, stood two ruby and gem decorated goblets fit for a king.

"Yes, I say this calls for dead babies washed down with a mixture of Sodomite vomit and piss. Tenth century, one of my favorite vintages."

"You are too kind, my Dark Lord."

"I prefer Morning Star. Suits my sterling character."

"Yes, of course my beautiful Morning Star." Asag choked out the words lathered in fear. This was typical of Lucifer, He enjoyed pushing the buttons of a worker. Lucifer knew Asag did not like formality nor did he prefer to drink such tainted human filth but here he was pushing it anyway. Oh Lucifer, you scalywag. For how can Asag deny his maker anything? More than just a shared cup of Hellish brew, Asag knew well that this, like everything else the Great Demon did, was a test. Asag was surprised that the babies were even offered to him. However, Asag, being of angelic descent, disdained such gruesome fare. To him all meat was just meat, but as a creature contorted into a fire-breathing abomination, everything just tasted like tar, so he had no complaints about the chewy children. And even if he had such misgivings, Asag was smart enough to know that to refuse such an offer from Morning Star Himself would like as not be the last thing he ever refused. So Asag reached his right claw out for one of the babies but Lucifer stopped him with a fart.

"No Fish Burner, you are my guest and as such I will not offer bare meat to my Antichrist. No, no, no, you deserve better."

Asag thought to himself that he should have known. The hot swamp parted like the Red Sea to reveal an overweight man in leather pulled by a chain attached to an Imp. The man was brought fearfully to the plate. The Imp inserted a large turkey baster up the human soul's ass and squeezed. The man shrieked. The suction of the baster pulled out human excrement infused with internal organs, pieces which he squirted all over the dead rotting baby bodies. The baby's eyes were wide open, blinking their Bambi-like lashes at the red dragon. They couldn't cry as rotten apples were stuffed in their tiny mouths. Snot dribbled their noses, as they tried to sniff up the snot it only added to the apple chucks spilling into their throats worsening their guttural coughing. Asag with his pinky up in the air Gabriel-style reached to pull one of the rotting apples from one of the living dead baby's mouth, a gesture of kindness. Lucifer looked on, amused. As the dirty, bloody, charred baby found its mouth unblocked it locked its eyes on Asag, smiling, It made the dreadful noises cats make when they fight in the alleys over a piece of stinking fish. The shrill cat scream emanating from the baby made the Fish Burner's scales crawl.

Asag looked at the puddle of pure evil. His stomach crawled around inside his belly.

"Now, you may eat."

All four of the new friends rode through the heart of Los Angeles as part of The World Naked Bike Ride. They were surrounded by the excitement of hundreds of naked bodies riding in the open air through town, more beautiful sunny nudist fun. An LAPD police escort ensured safety, letting the bicyclists wiz past intersections without getting turned into road pizza. Body painted riders covered in sorts of all crazy designs flanked the streets and sat mounted peddling away on their bikes. WNBR in LA had been happening for years. It was glorious and brave and fun and free of spirit. The World's Naked Bike Ride was decorated with crazy hats, wigs, messages written on bodies, cars tooting their horns and folks hollering up some fun. There were also those who were angry. Somebody threw something thinking it was some sort of "parade for faggots" because they are ignorant in the true sense of the word. When an event of this open manner happens on Earth, this sort of glitch is commonplace. Humans could be brave, and humans could be miserly and fearful of the unknown. Cops earn their wages on days like this because you just don't know what kind of whack-job is lurking around the corner waiting to become famous at the expense of innocent passersby. Arrests happen here and there, and the parade of nude cyclists rides past. This reminds D'mon of Hell somehow, he wasn't quite sure of the parallel, perhaps it is the herding of the sheep not know how much peril they are in at any given moment or perhaps because they are all exposed and judgment is waiting to descend? Perhaps it was because he simply liked it here and at times, or maybe even for the most part, he liked it in Hell as well.

A quick glance at Jessica peddling beside him and D'mon's mind was finished drifting for the moment. She was sweaty and panting, her legs working hard, he liked watching her. Freckles.

D'mon's penis fell asleep and he couldn't feel it. *What the fuck?* the ex demon thought. At the checkpoint where the bikers stop for a break, he shook it to wake it up and the cops thought he was masturbating and wandered over to talk to him.

"Drop the gun, son." Officer Windham ordered, trying not to laugh. Today was a paid 'off day' for the stout cop. He knew this gig was pretty easy for the most part, free money, but there was always some joker that had to make things weird. And then there was the fucking Hell hot flack vest.

"Excuse me? I, ah, ha-ha. Yes sir, I was just . . ."

"I don't even wanna know about it, pal," the cop said shifting his belt, adjusting his baton, "Nude not Lewd. Lewd is a crime." Jessica, Chrissy and David all rushed over to explain the situation, eventually the sweating cop laughed recommending a seat with a hole in it for blood circulation.

"I got the same affliction myself." Officer Windham said through his think mustache. D'mon hated mustaches; they reminded him of President Duulexebub. Fuck that guy.

The foursome rode on for some time, enjoying the company, the public nakedness, and just the plain coolness of it all. D'mon and Jessica shared some lovey dovey moments stolen between ordering food, laughing with David and Chrissy and everyone else. This was life, eh? Pretty cool shit. D'mon even rented them a bicycle built for two so they could fumble around and be cheesy as Hell. He saw her eyeing the twin seat bicycle and some new feeling within him drove him to get it for her. His new emotions helped guide him in combination with his demon's wit. This new software was changing his hard drive or at least that's how he figured it. D'mon realized that this was her family, nudists and body acceptance culture. He could see such love and humanity. Non-judgement. He felt bad for how miserable Jessica had been when he first met her. That life and Heaven and Hell made something and someone this beautiful so distorted. For the first time in a long time Damien-ki Zakire Monteloflobe was truly and completely happy.

Empty mouthwash containers littered the office of Earth's future Antichrist. Ray Ma Ching pushed aside bottles as he entered the doorway to his office.

"How was it? Does he know?"

"He knows, of course he fucking knows. He knows everything. Fuck." The Fish Burner finished and threw his eighth container at the wall. Ray wasn't exactly sure why the large red dragon was doing this, perhaps all that fire breathing was wreaking havoc on his gums, but the more likely answer was something Ray was probably better off not knowing since Asag had just returned from a meeting with a creature that made Charlie Mansion look like Mahatma Gandhi.

Asag was very agitated and slightly unwilling to do as Lucifer had commanded him because he had a great deal of work to put together numbers and factors to project exactly how this will all play out. The Fish Burner knew Lucifer was capable of acting before the seventh day, but laziness is the Morning Stars Achilles

Heel… next to vanity, he is sitting in his Lake of Fire 'watching TV without a remote' as Lucifer had put it. And scheming.

"I am torn here. If Lucifer gets the slightest hint of treasonous intensions from me, he will destroy me without hesitation. I must believe D'mon will do the right thing." said the large demon ironically.

"Oh, but of course, sir. If anyone around here knows talent, it's you and you trained D'mon to be the best. It would be impossible for him to fail because it is impossible for you to fail, sir." Ray wanted to laugh but showed no outward sighs at all, he too was on a slippery slope. Ray Ma Ching's private aspirations were grandiose and grossly over-reaching. "Sir, please do not be stressing about this. Your time is best focused elsewhere. YOU are the Anti-Christ, sir." Asag needed to hear this even if Ray's words were poison.

"Ray, you are a good guy. Thank you."

"Why, thank *you*, sir. Besides, D'mon showed such distain for you, Asag, you shouldn't belittle yourself to beg anything from Lucifer on his behalf. YOU are, as I have so loyally pointed out, are the Anti-Christ of this world! Have some self-respect! You're the boss!"

Asag thought that it sounded a tad overzealous of Ray to say such things, but the compliments far exceeded the pep talk. Pep talks were doled out *by* the Fish Burner, not *to* the Fish Burner. But Ray's point struck at the heart of Asag's ego so what the Hell?

"Sir, I will again return to try and talk some common sense into Damien-ki Zakire Monteloflobe for the sake of Hell and every-thing. He is just as torn as you are and needs guidance which I will provide on your behalf while you hold down the fort, sir."

"Please, Ray, plead with D'mon to return and put an end to this political catastrophe, this religious cluster fuck."

"Of course sir, you can count on me." cackled Ray Ma Ching as he left his Boss's sweltering office.

NINE

The wind blew softly as two bodies clung to one another in a hammock between two trees in the yard of David Ladd. David was an old man now but in his youth was a founder of the Southern California Bare Bodies Federation. In the nudist world it's the SCBBF. Since they were a non-landed club, they did events at rented-out bowling alleys, art galleries, and private residences like his own back yard. Hours earlier it had been a bustle of over a hundred naked bodies all enjoying his pool, his hot tub and his food. Now there was only a few guests that remained. These few would be spending the night. Jessica looked at D'mon's face. They were soaking in Old David's hot tub. She traced the features and contours of his face with her fingers, his nose, his lips. She couldn't believe it had been only seven days.

"Seven days," the famous writer said. D'mon's blue eyes shot open at once. Jessica stared into his them, "Tomorrow will be my *seventh* day." She almost sang the word seventh.

This was no joke D'mon thought to himself.

"Thinking of setting the deal on fire?" His face was stern. "I have the parchment if you want it? Do you want it, Jessica?"

"You know I can't do that. I'm to start the book tour in a few days, plus I don't want to die. Dying would just suck and if there is gonna be any sucking around here its gonna be with you and me."

"Anything else?"

She knew he was serious when he didn't smile at her innuendos. Pulling damp strands red hair from her face she kissed him hard on the mouth. "Yes, yes there is. You don't just have my soul, you have my heart too. I think I love you, D'mon." He looked surprised that she said it. "What? So yeah, I don't want this ever to end. I don't want to burn the contract."

"Then don't. Relax hon." He held her close. The smell of her wet hair, her sun tinted flesh, her sweet breath, it all entranced him. He was happier than he could ever remember being in all his long, long life.

"Did you just call me 'hon?"

"Ha, shut it. Most people who sell their souls become at risk for bad things like possession or a deep, indescribable feeling of loss of self that can't assuaged, and that's because they are separated from what makes them human. You aren't separated from that part of you, it's near you and always will be, because I'm here. You didn't lose your soul, it just got . . . transplanted."

"You're right, I didn't lose my soul, I found my soulmate."

This hit D'mon like a happy ton of mushy bricks. He could feel the happiness making the back of his eyeballs hot. They kissed then in such a passionate way that it was as if time itself were standing still. The wind stopped, birds stopped, time stood still, literally.

"Well, well, look at you, Fuck Machine, you dinky ding dong." Ray Ma Ching floated above the Jacuzzi swatting at the air as he fell less than gracefully near the couple.

"What is it now Ray? Everything alright?"

"Well, let's think about this, we have a lowly demon from Hell walking the Earth with a contraband human soul that he stole stuffed inside of him, cannnnnoodling with a fleshy fresh cunt. What do you think? Is everything alright?"

"Watch how you talk about Jessica, you little shit."

"What? How I talk about . . . Are you fucking kidding me, your majesty? Have you lost your God damned mind, Damien-ki Zakire Monteloflobe? Jesus-fucking-Christ-on-a-stick-on-Sunday."

"Ray, I told you I wasn't going back. That's it. No more." D'mon moved gently away from his paused girlfriend, a look of absolute ecstasy on her beautiful, freckled face. "You think I'm a nice guy, well I'm not a nice guy. I am the top Soul Trader in Hell for a reason. It's because I know all the rules. You can't send an army to drag me back and I know that." D'mon grabbed the little fluttery Cherub and squeezed him hard, dragging him back towards the swimming pool. "As long as I have this soul in my possession Hell is going to have to wait a very long time to see me, or her. I found the vacation I was promised and I'm enjoying me some Californication. You should try it out, Ray. Really. Here, let me help you cool off ya little turd." D'mon dragged Ray into the pool. He had to push hard to dunk Ray's head in the still liquid but managed it. Ray's screams became garbled. D'amon finally pulled him out.

"Okay, okay, shit. Shit, okaaaaaay."

"No more visits, no more pauses in the time stream, no harassment or I will stuff my size thirteen foot into your droopy little shitter. Understood?"

"I had a message from Asag, you remember him, right? The Fish Burner? The guy that helped train you to be the best."

D'mon stopped to listen.

"Asag says that he's proud of you and you have the blessing of Hell to stay here as long as you wish."

"You're full of shit, twerp."

"No, I swear."

"You lie."

"No, Asag met with Lucifer. Everything's cool now."

Grabs him and went to dunk him again. "You being straight

with me you fat fucking Chink? Why? Why is everything cool? Speak, bitch."

"It just is dammit. After today you won't see me again!"

"Promise it."

"I goddamn fucking promise." He let Ray go. Ray rubbed his neck looking at him. "You got an attitude problem man, you're a hothead. Hello, A loose cannon." Ray's accent made D'mon laugh. He wasn't racist, but it was amusing nonetheless.

"If I ever see you again, I'll fuck you up. Bad. Ray, I mean it. I'll fuck you up. If you truly enjoy fluttering around with those wings of yours I suggest that you fuck off before I rip them off."

Ray looked in his eyes. He knew he meant it. D'mon say the fear in the fat little cherubs eyes and grinned a menacing grin. There was a loud pop and Ray was gone.

When time picked back up, D'mon was next to Jessica again. She asked him, "Is everything okay?" He looked deep into her eyes, to that sparkle of all that was right in the universe.

"From here on out, things will only get better for both of us. I love you too."

He said it and he meant it.

Representatives from all the Hells in all the galaxies were present and accounted for. Creatures that varied in sizes from humanoid to microscopic, to blue whale size, to the stature of the sun all fit into one size-less cosmically celestial conference room. They varied as well in esthetics, scary, plantlike, gross, scary, evil, unearthly. Some beasts did not even look remotely like life as we know it. There were creatures that were basically giant eyeballs with no other recognizable limbs floated around blinking at the other company. There were creatures that you couldn't tell their eyes from their cocks or if it had either at all. This place was filled with such oddities that were the stuff of nightmares in every plane of existence in every dimension, from every conceivable time frame. Asag kept checking the door to his section waiting for Ray Ma Ching to arrive before his presentation. As Antichrist of Hell he was to give a status report on the situation of that world. The skies above rippled in red and constant torment.

Lucifer sat far below the proceedings, bubbling and rolling over himself with souls speckled all over his unholy hide. Disgusting fat shitty garbage, nothing pleasant or redeeming about it. Each rep takes their turn giving updates standing on a protruding platform with holes in it to see Lucifer underneath. The Morning Star was far away from this place but with the infernal magic and science of the boundaries of space, time and the ethereal *Everything*, he looked on from where it all converged, here, at his fingertips or claws or whatever he had. If unpleased Lucifer might invoke, in simplistic human worlds for you idiot humans that are reading this book, that the 'End of Days' is a go, bringing Earth into yet another stage of the cosmic cocoon. Representatives of other worlds where Armageddon had already occurred stood by curiously. Some demonic delegates present had already been active Anti-Christs in their own milieu not just *in waiting* to become one as Asag was. The wild plethora of the highest-ranking demons from around Infinity were talking and arguing when the Archangels suddenly appeared. Again, no trumpets, no pyro, no nothing, they were just fucking there.

Mical and zadZiel came down from the plane of Heaven to follow up on their earlier warning as it is the seventh day in just a scant few Earth hours. The Angel of Mercy stood and surveyed the masses of Hellish things. He was not disgusted nor disdainful nor looking down his nose but rather he was simply indifferent.

"We have made His intensions clear and fair. We expect His wishes complied with and fulfilled to completion." zadZiel's handsome Clooneyish face looked from side to side, his voice was everywhere, "Comply and there shall be mercy. Failure to comply will ensure an unpleasant trip to oblivion."

The demons mumbled. So many of them combined sounded like a volcano erupting or a planet exploding. The giant eyed PusPusBag made an awful sound translating to something blasphemous. Before the round white creature could finish its rant Mical waved his hand and the creature was gone on its way to an apparently unpleasant Heavenly oblivion. The endless amount of remaining demons grumbled even louder but about nothing directly sacrilegious.

"There are still several hours left of your seven days to comply. Please, do not make the same mistake your colleague PusPusBag did."

"I care not for excuses nor do I care to speak with the highest of underlings. Lucifer, you know my mind and my will. We were once brothers, so I grant you a boon I would grant to no other. You mistook my kindness for weakness once a very long time ago. I beg you not to make the same mistake twice, my brother." Mical's voice engulfed the highest most Infernal room in Infinity.

"Please your holiness, this is not the doing of Lucifer." A small voice said from far beneath the Archangel. Ray Ma Ching was lucky to be in this room which was way above his pay grade. It was brass ring time for the little conniving cherub.

"I am here to speak to chiefs not Indians little repugnant one. Be gone," commanded Mical. Was that a tone of condescension Ray heard in the Archangel's voice?

"Please your grace, I have vital information. I have news of contempt! A celestial conspiracy involving the Anti-Christ and the demon you seek! Perhaps the information I have will also help mend the broken relationship between you and your brother, Morning Star. I speak the truth, I am a cherub after all." Asag was thunderstruck. He could not believe his dragon ears. He, Asag, was being called out publicly by his employee, a fucking cherub for fucks sake! The notion of Ray helping him in some eccentric way was quickly fleeting.

"Speak, cherub," commanded Mical.

"The Moring Star understands about how painful the Great Fall was. He would never allow it to happen again.

As much as Lucifer wanted to snuff out this inconsequential nobody, suddenly, Ray Ma Ching was on his radar. This had better be fuckin' good. Morning Star rumbled dangerously in his tub of flame.

"Where's D'mon? Damien-ki Zakire Monteloflobe is still free on the earthly plane fueled by a soul that he has stolen from the Morning Star." Ray had the spotlight in the toughest room EVER!

"This is fucking outrageous! I . . .," growled the red dragon.

"Silence, Asag the Fish Burner. Speak when spoken to." Mical didn't even look at Asag whilst his voice penetrated everything. Did Ray fail Asag or solidify himself? To say that Ray Ma Ching was out for himself was an understatement of Biblical proportions.

"Asag the Fish Burner, the Admissions Director of the Eternal Infernal realm, the Anti-Christ-In-Waiting is a giant big fat PUSSY!" Ray felt mentally orgasmic as he liberated himself of those words that had been stabbing inside of him for so long, "I have tried my best despite Asag's unwillingness to go fix this diabolical situation."

"You little mother fuc . . .," Asag lunged for the small Asian cherub but was frozen into the ether by the wave zadZeil's hand.

"Consider yourself lucky Fish Burner, if it was I waving my hand you would not be frozen here, you would be gone." Mical's voice echoed into the red dragon's ear holes. Lucifer's repugnant body of rape, sodomy and lamentation looked on from the Lake of Fire at this cosmic kangaroo court.

Things continued to get heated and the endless hoard of demon cabinet members continued to rumble.

"What proof ya got?" blurted Kopsazxc, a large demon with millions of penises covering its body along with a drooling unkempt vagina mouth.

"Yes. What proof have you, little cherub?" Mical inquired.

"I found THIS at the bottom of one of Asag's fish tanks!" Ray pulls a satchel out of thin air. His little piggy's hand reached in and retrieved the Angel Gabriel's severed head. The head had been most grievously mistreated. The angel's skull was riddled with charred fuck holes and slime. Mical and zadZiel both still looked indifferent but then they booth smiled. This couldn't be good. These smiles weren't 'tee hee that was funny' smiles, more like the 'we are gonna fuck your shit up royally' kind.

Everyone was in disbelief. The collective sigh could be heard around Infinity reaching all the way to Oblivion.

"This travesty notwithstanding, I do believe in an eye for an eye." Mical grimaced, "Fish Burner, do you know the difference between the unknown tortures of Hell versus the unknown tortures of Heaven?" Mical smiled his grim, mirthless smile yet again, "We are justified in anything we choose to do." Spoken like a true psychopath.

"He killed an Angel of Heaven?" shouted Defgrrrratwampafu-uukt simultaneously from all three of his gaping mouths as his tentacles changed color due to his escalated emotions.

"Gods gentle hero! An emissary of God!" Ray pointed out, "He's even in The Holy Earth Bible! Several times!"

The demons continued to murmur. Lucifer pondered the situation whilst staring at the endless torn and punished bodies that he was comprised of. Ray was awful and dirty and terrible; Lucifer's new favorite flavor of the week.

"There are things that we will not work out today and there are things that you, my dear brother, that Morning Star will recognize." Lucifer bellowed. When he spoke about himself in the third person it was usually to spew some tyrannical garbage. "I am appalled at the actions or lack thereof from my employee, Asag, the Fish Burner!" The Morning Star beamed a bright red light from his wrenched gnarled fingers directly at Asag, who screamed in agony. Lucifer smiled. "Let us turn up the volume, shall we?" With the wave of the Devil's claws the Fish Burner was immediately swarmed with vile ratigans. A few moments passed which seemed like an eternity for Asag, then, suddenly, with the snap of the Morning Star's fingers Asag was gone.

"Is he destroyed, brother?" Mical asked.

"No," Lucifer answered, "This wretch has been lost to a prison until I decide how exactly I want to send him to oblivion. If you play with fire long enough you get burned. You taught me that lesson well, brother."

Lucifer looked the chubby Asian cherub as he spoke to the Archangels and the cabinet of the highest demons. Ray bit his lip trying hard not to smile thinking, *Lucifer just looked at me! He totally just looked a ME!*

TEN

In the beginning there was God. God is known by many names in many tongues in many worlds, but His reasoning and His existentialism was known only to His Own Self. Why were there such horrors in every universe? Why not just eradicate the evil and create only lands of goodness and prosperity? Why allow a child to starve to death if there could be a way to save her? Why? God sits and waits.

God's house was seen from afar by all the saved souls, the various light fueled beings such as Dions, Papadons, Reids, and some Cherubs who hadn't defected to Hell's Admissions. Flutters as well as other species of Angels and the league of angels above them, known as the powerful Archangels were all a part of God's grand plan. The house of God was not an ivory cathedral or a mammoth pyramid but rather one large, white, pure cube set high on top of a staircase that could take some beings a lifetime to climb. There He remained, in His house while all of Heaven awaits His next move, His next creations, and in the meantime as He meditates in slumber, His few proclamations are told through Mical, who would messenger the note through Gabriel, although that Archangel had recently been missing. Tensions about the absent angel were high and if you rode Mical you could find yourself staring at a bull in a cosmic china shop very quickly.

Glistening and gleaming, Mical stood tall and proud with his red toga flowing in the sunny atmosphere. He rarely exposed his golden tipped wings, but sometimes he would stretch them wide to show the souls within Heaven who was watching over them. He mostly kept them tucked close to his back out of humility and as a military tactic to keep his person safe from stealthier attackers. An arrow suddenly piercing an exposed wing might make the different between winning and losing a battle. He did not have his weapons for war on him as this was as casual as he would get feeling safe in Heaven but make no mistake he was always on guard. Next to him was zadZiel fretting over this recent business.

"So, we are to follow through on this then, brother?"

"Naturally, I laid it out to God and He spoke to me as He does. His words were 'signs pointing to yes' and that is really all we need to know." Mical explained to zadZiel who then nodded.

"Then I shall gather the other Archangels, they will be proud to stand by you in yet another . . ."

"That is not necessary, I don't want to risk anything befalling them in such a simple mission. We will instead arm the golden falcons, we've had them long enough."

"The falcons! They are built for terrible war. God cried when He made them, wishing His creation's free will would never force His hand to employ them. What dear brother will we use as the power source?"

"Since we are going to Earth to bring back an Earthbound Soul Trader I think it's only just to power them with some thetans we have lying around up here."

"Thetans, brother you're astounding. I didn't know that we had any human souls just lying around. They earned their time here by living a wholesome life down there."

"Wholesome? Life? Did you not hear my words to my dear Morning Star's colleagues? The only difference between the goings-on of Heaven and Hell are that we are justified. I believe this in my heart of hearts to be exactly that." Mical looked down past his flock to the scurrying ants in the living realm. "What's a lifespan down there? One hundred years, max? Let's compare that to an Angel or a demon? I don't think they deserve any of this. You want to have your desert you've gotta eat your veggies as they say." Mical opened the door to the cloud car. It was a faster ride than walking or wings in Heaven. They could do whatever their imaginations allowed but always found it amusing to create efficient parodies of what the talking apes made. A car created in Heaven would never need servicing or a transmission replacement. Nothing on Earth worked right not just thanks to Hell but by human's own shoddy work. Greedy idiots, that was their status quo.

"I don't follow what you're saying."

"Get in the Mobly, let's head to the Thetan playground." Once both were inside, Mical took control of the zip controls and away they flashed. Below them they saw various versions of Heaven created in different eyes for different beings. Mical cringed at the Middle Eastern levels, so disturbing, always seventy-two virgins to every long-bearded camel jockey. So chauvinistic. How in the Hell did those clowns qualify their demeaning asses into this lovely place? Oh, God, your infinite wisdom it eludes me. The Valhalla level was far more amusing to the Archangel.

He appreciated their straightforwardness. Fight bravely and go to a better place; the strongest survive in glory. It was noble in a primitive way. Ironically there was a large sect of atheists and agnostics within the clouds. Believing in nothing but trying to be nice to their fellow man at least got brownie points in the common-sense department. Let's face it, there has been some evil shit done in the name of 'religion' which Hell and its agents had a big part in. This was a sore spot for the angels. A stain on their honor to be associated with infernal cunts like Pope Innocent, or Borgia and so many other well dressed entitled tyrants. Mical always enjoyed the look on the faces of would-be holy men as they were denied access thru the Pearly Gates but instead given VIP passes to the hottest club in town. The angels snickered at that Hell joke time and time again, it never got old.

When they got to the vast space in Heaven reserved for human shades that had died and rose through the clouds to meet their maker it was all about them. They were waited on by Angels poolside in some areas and read philosophy in others. There was joyful singing and, yes, even harps. zadZiel did not like to see what he refered to as the Yard. It rubbed him the wrong way. Different factions of various denominations playing basketball or lifting weights or just standing around smoking cigarettes that were good for you, but all segregated looking down at one another. The Yard was similar to Times Square where all the Burrows met and conjoined. The standard issue togas were offered but not mandatory, some would rather dress in their 'I love Zenu' t-shirts or their snappy Nazi uniforms or whatever tickled their fancy. This was a place where you couldn't be hurt by another soul even if they tried. This was a place where injuries did not exist unless doled out by someone of angelic stature. Angels would police the area observing all sorts of cultures and what those souls would consider to be Heaven, so it pleased everyone. Even amongst this pleasantness and revelry some looked bored. Even zadZiel saw this and was perplexed at how humans could always find a way to be discontent.

"How can it be so? We give them all they could want? Companions, family, hobbies and we ask nothing of them in return." Mical and zadZiel were reminded of what Asag had said about the ant farm he had in his youth. "Some need to be freed to roam."

"Why not just grab this Damien-ki Zakire Monteloflobe as the humans he is surrounded by slumber, why do any of their lives need to be ended?"

"The demon is like a disease and we are taking measures to

assure that we excise the wound from Earth. Plus…this is God's will, not mine." zadZiel nodded, dejectedly.

"We need the souls that got in on a curve. The 'barely made-its' is who we are looking for. If you ask me they all qualify but our Father doesn't see it that way, so we will respect His opinions and wishes. We need some interactions with these… humans," Mical could barely say the word, "Possibly to decipher who chooses to go and why they… Well, let's just say that I'm am sure the majority of them will be happy to simply stretch their feet. It's not like it was a hard sell for them to get stoned to death for stealing a loaf of stale bread or burn someone at the stake because they were maaaaybe a witch. Idiots."

"Ewwww, look over there, some large Negros from the slavery days. They are good workers. Malnourished and over-worked and they still grew up big and strong, just not the sharpest knives in the drawer."

"Perfect," Mical's voice was heard by all. He didn't especially care. "Grab anyone one wearing a Swastika or has one tattooed on their person. They love to kill things!"

Time flew along timelessly. The human ghosts began training at the base of the stairs to the throne of almighty God. Mical went up to inquire if they could leave yet. A short while passed as the Archangel cames down with Gods reply. "Reply is hazy, try again."

zadZiel thought that was odd, but who is he to question God or the top Archangel.

Mical cheats slightly by touching all the shade's foreheads, giving each of them a piece of Heavenly inspiration. In layman's terms: Mind Control. Mical waved his hands and the giant golden falcons rose from the surrounding clouds like a cloud of starlings over a Midwestern field. The human souls got inside the five thousand looming birds of prey. The birds were actually animated golden falcon statues with vicious beaks and horrible talons. They need to practice for battle as they possess the vehicles and soar and fly about. Mical goes back up and again returns with an answer form God. "Ask again later." The Archangel was frustrated as he watched the celestial falcons practice aerial dogfight tactics.

This was the happiest day ever for Jessica Ro, the soon to be best-selling author. Her agent said that there was a huge bidding war over the book rights earlier and now an even bigger war over the film rights and the book was not even released yet. Plus, fan sites are popping up just at the ideas she presents. Jessica Ro, writer guru genius fakir! So original... Marvel has offered to change the names of The Fantastic Four! That was a good thing because Jessica really did not want to go with her secondary choices: Clark, Bruce, Diana and Lex.

"Only one way to celebrate all this. Let's go to DISNEY-LAND!" screamed the redheaded writer as she jumped into the lap of her lover, Damien-ki Zakire Monteloflobe, now legally (or legally enough) known as D'mon Rhodes. The ex-Demon had tinkered with D'mon Wayans but thought it sounded too familiar to . . . you know?

David interrupted while fidgeting with his smart phone.

"Guys! I have a friend that works there and can get y'all in free. Chrissy, D'mon, Jessica! The happiest place on Earth! Woot! Woot!

D'mon and Jessica were very much in love and were planning a long happy life together, the term 'soulmate' never before seemed so fitting until now. This was Heaven for the former employee of Hell. All that really matters is the present, right now, plus Hell gave its blessing and Heaven is full of such pacifists. They played with predictions of what futures they would create together, invent their own publishing house, *Ro & Rhodes Books*.

The pure white skies of the blank page of creation were marked by golden streaks flying every which way. Yelling and thundering noises were heard as many took to mock fighting with each other. Scrapes and claws and biting was happening as zadZiel waited patiently at the base of the stairs.

"These are falcons, not ducks you morons," Mical blasted.

Even with Mical's warrior nature, zadZiel knew that God's Mercy was just and any life that might be taken would not be in vain but to better the predestination of His holy will. Still zadZiel wondered why they were instructed not to alert the other Archangels as a demon that was on the loose beyond its boundaries was considered blasphemy of the highest order. Furthermore, to use human souls in a bloodthirsty display of aggression seemed morally ambiguous at best. zadZiel could see a mob of Nazi soldiers, 1940's mobsters, ninjas, negro slaves and some Roman guards flank Mical has he reached the top of the stairs. Mical did not stop before entering the Pearly Gates (which incidentally was not actually made of pearl but rather some unknown unearthly ore).

The vast empty room had a white and black-checkered floor. The ceiling was arched, but so high that the painting that covered it was much too far away to be discerned. The sound of doves could be heard yet they were no doves in sight. The mob stood dumb-founded soaking up the room in which the almighty Creator dwelt. Mical approached an empty crystal throne at its center. It was so pure the translucency of its material made it almost see through. The Archangel reached his hand out from his shining red silks for a response and got: "Signs point to yes." Finally, Mical received the answer he was faithfully waiting on. He looked at the Magic Eight-ball in his hands.

Mical eyes were now replaced with fire. The Nazis and ninjas and Negros alike bowed their heads. Although the mob had histori-cally been either misguidedly doing what they were told, or mind-lessly fulfilling a misplaced sense of honor, or just forced into it, they all were ready for more service. The creature in the red toga with the fiery eyes was no dictator, nor emperor, nor plantation owner. he was the liaison to God and they would follow him.

"Praise be it to the Word of our Lord and Almighty God, amen," A titanic chorus of 'Amens!' swelled from the newly recruited celestial troops.

ELEVEN

The golden webbing began to wrap itself around the edges of one of California's greatest attractions. The space between California Adventure and Disneyland couldn't have been further apart this day. The comfort webbings gave a sense of indifference to the customers not yet inside and had them turning either to leave completely or go to only the California Adventure side. As the webbings tightened it sealed the fate of those still inside. It was beautiful and awe inspiring to look at, but little did people know how much of a prison it would become. The skies opened, and golden death reigned from on high. In moments the shrieking cries of the golden falcons tore the air as the Raptors of God descended upon the tourists and Disney fans. Fuck Mickey Mouse, run for your life! Families and friends, crew and executives, cast members and mascots, college kids in giant frumpy suits clamored to escape the walls of talons and vicious beaks. Goofy got his big stuffed head torn clean off not to mention Jeff Jackson's head as well (Jeff was the nineteen-year-old college freshman inside the costume).

Horrible things were happening everywhere and to everyone, young and old. It was as if they were all in line for the last and most gruesome ride of their pathetic little lives. The golden talons would be the last things many people would see this day, God fearing or otherwise. The sharp golden hooks would be through you before you could blink. Crimson stained claws dissected people from their privates to the top of their skulls. The concrete ground looked as if blood had rained down from the Heavens, but it had not, it was the coming from the endless amount of scurrying victims at the happiest place on God's green earth. Behind them all came Mical in full Archangel battle armor and flaming sword two sizes too big. His golden tipped wings had a giant expanse, the under layer of feathers was black. It was not mentioned in the Good Book that Mical's wings resembled that of a giant raven for PR's sake. Hell wasn't the only celestial business with a great creative staff at their disposal.

The train, the Halloween decorations, a torn-off Mickey Mouse head rolled by. This scene was not the most ideal location for coherent thought. Chaos was in full swing. Potbellied fan boys could swear they just saw Ric Flair and George Clooney swoop out of the sky killing as many people as they could. Mical's golden armor and bleach blond locks were stained as red as his toga from the blood of the ignorant, or the innocent, or whomever.

"Worry not, my children, we come with Gospel, good news for you all," zadZiel bellowed loudly calling to all who would hear him. "Today many of you will see the glory of God and the rest of you, my flock, will still have time to ask for forgiveness." People all around were having their intestines pulled out and their heads split open. Women and children were crying as the little ones were ripped from their parents and flown away then dropped turning into splattering puddles far below as they hit the unforgiving cement. "God's mercy awaits you all," zadZiel pronounced with open outstretched arms.

Some people dropped to their knees while surrounded by torn bodies as others ran looking for an exit. The falcons swooped down onto the folks praying as they were easy targets. Mical didn't mind the falcon's overzealous nature, they were after all just sheep following their shepherd's orders. *'C'est la vie'* the Archangel thought to himself.

The baby-blue and gold turrets surrounding the Haunted Mansion were washed in the blood of its patrons. The large Ferris wheel could no longer spin due to the number of severed limbs clogging up its hydraulics. The cotton candy drooped soggily weighted with plasma from ravaged employees and the Walt Disney statue hand had impaled a factory worker, Juan, a father of two. He hung limp in the wind with Walt's pointing hand sticking thru a gaping opening in his chest cavity. Mickey and Minnie were dead, Goofy was dead, Pluto was dead, Donald was a dead duck alright, and the whole fucking place was definitely a wonder world.

Security was kicking themselves about Disney's 'no gun' policy! Fuck sakes! The boss has one anyway. Charlie ran to go get his Glock Safe Action. He scrabbled in his desk frantically. Charlie was sucking wind, this was all just too much to process! Why the fuck was George Clooney and Ric Flair and a bunch of golden geese attacking the happiest place on Earth? The bullets dropped through his fat fingers, his hands were shaking terribly. Charlie wasn't going to go out like this, he was going to be the hero and get to be on TV and get interviewed by Oprah, Dave and Ellen. He would get invited to exclusive Hollywood parties where he would bang supermodels and porn stars just like Charlie Sheen did! They would hang out and get into bar fights together and be known as the two Charlies! Fuck those geese! They didn't know who they were messing with! Charlie finally got the magazine in and a couple of spare 9mm clips in his pocket for good measure. The tubby, balding security guard stormed out of the bright colored and now blood-soaked office firing ammunition into the golden death.

"Charlie is here, you fuckers! I got your golden goose riiiiiii-ight here. Fuckin' birds!" His fixed steel sights helped him land almost every round from his mag, but the bad news was they bounced off the birds of prey like tennis balls. One stray 9mm bullet hit zadZiel in the temple. The Archangel started to fall. "Holy shit I shot George Clooney! I knew you fuckin' actors had to have made a deal with the devil to be so God damn famous and good looking!"

zadZiel was just stunned. He heard the security guard's words between the ringing in his head. 'holy shit', 'deal with the devil', 'God damned famous', none of these words sat well with the Archangel. He felt like he had been knocked down in the same way awful children would hit a bird with a rock. This metaphor was surprisingly accurate.

"Do you repent?" zadZiel asked Charlie.

"Fuck you, Clooney," Charlie held down the trigger, his weapon pointed directly at the Archangel's face. Click. Click. Click. Click. Nothing. Charlie was empty. He through his piece down and put up his dukes. With one wave of zadZiel's hand Charlie's decapitated head was soaring thru the bloody sky amongst the devastating geese that were actually falcons.

David and D'mon had been holding the place in line leading up to the 'It's a Small World' ride. It was a day full of people having fun and they'd already seen the animatronic characters pop out from the wall twice.

"Don't mention it to Chrissy but I really hated that last ride."

"Mr. Toad's Wild Ride?"

"Yeah, so let me get this straight, it's a ride at Disneyland for kids?"

"Sure." D'mon agreed.

"So, we get in a goofy little car which is fun, then somewhere in the ride we get hit by a train and go to Hell." D'mon looked at him fully aware that he had taken note of that particular part as well. "Hit by a train and sent to Hell. The End. That's the ride." D'mon stoked his dreadlocks in bewilderment.

The former demon laughed. He felt so at home with these strangers. He was able to just be a guy that didn't have to wear devil horns or a red tux, just jeans and a t-shirt like any other guy. This was great.

"It should be a punishment for bad kids, like if they steal a giant pickle they have to ride the go to Hell ride." Chrissy piped up as she and Jessica were making their way back over to the men.

"Hey, don't tell her, I know she loves that stupid ride."

The girls joined them.

Wasn't the Toad ride great?" Chrissy looked at D'mon.

"You know it." D'mon held on to Jessica by the waist. He suddenly remembered she wasn't wearing any panties under her yellow summer sundress. They moved up a few steps in line.

"Something I noticed in Disney films recently." Everyone looked at David. "What's with the moms?

"What do you mean?" Chrissy asked.

"Well I was watching The Little Mermaid and she's got a chubby dad but no mom. Then I was watching Beauty and the Beast and again chubby dad but no mom, so I put on Aladdin, he's dating that Jasmine who has a chubby dad but where's the mom? Disney is against moms I think." David speculated, "Is Walt Disney the devil incarnate?"

"That's crazy," Chrissy said thinking to herself, "Wait, what about Bambi? She has a mom."

"Yeah, they finally put a mom in the movie and they blow her fucking brains out." David added, "Walt Satan!"

"Pixar is no better, like I want to see the goddamn cycle of life at the beginning of 'Up'? Geez, and remember 'Finding Nemo'?" They all nodded except D'mon, apparently Disney films aren't popular in Hell.

"Okay, so *Finding Nemo* has a happy fish family at the beginning, then right away some monster comes out of the depths of the ocean, eats the mom first, then eats ninety-nine of the one hundred little fish egg babies leaving the dad with one gimpy fish son left, then the movie treats the dad like he's an asshole for being a little over protective of his last kid in the world," David ranted.

"I think you're taking cartoons to seriously. No more cartoons for you for a while, Mr. Man," fired the laughing Jessica.

"I think we'll be watching lots of cartoons soon," Chrissy pats her tummy where the bun is in the oven.

Meanwhile back at the Dungeon of Doom.

Mical swung his fiery sword through people right and left. He swung at women and children eventually stopping as the crowd were just more and more bodies, so he chose to fly back up into the Heavens. From there he called on a swift page from the Old Testament. Sulfur came down and man, woman and child alike began to change to salt. Pillars of salt people grew in population. All ashy clumps of screaming salt.

zadZiel rose up to meet his celestial brother in arms. Mical looked him over making sure he was okay. He wanted this whole mess to just be over.

"Pillars of salt. At least their suffering will end now even quicker, brother." Mical brushed off the comments and hollered toward his flying assault.

"Check every ride, every attraction, falcons. The demon hides among you."

As all the little mechanical people representing all nations of the Earth danced and sang, D'mon felt something stir inside him. D'mon and Jessica sat in the back of a boat that moved along slowly through the water. Jessica was taking pictures and in front of them sat the couple that had embraced him as one of their own in their nudist tribe. The faces of the indigenous peoples began to blur and contort reminding him of the tortured souls in Hell. The souls he himself put there, forced to Ro the Styx. Was that a giant golden falcon? Noticing the freak-out Jessica stopped taking pictures and held D'mon close.

"All these people," D'mon finally understood the value of human life.

"You saved me." Jessica gripped him tight, her eyes widening in disbelief.

David and Chrissy started to freak out as blood started washing into the It's A Wonderful Life exit. Body parts rolled in on top the crimson tide. D'mon started to think. This was all his fault. How did he ever think the Devil or God would let him get away with his freedom?

"Save us D'mon!" Jessica joined David and Chrissy in their well-warranted hysteria. D'mon's human emotions were inter-twined with his devious demon mind. He needed to find a solution, or this would all be over before it started. The dark-skinned former Soul Trader needed a miracle. The irony of this situation was not lost on him. The light in the distance was unbearably bright, a Heavenly ray of sunshine breathing new life ahead, except just the opposite was the case! Angelic irony was everywhere, and it was a bitch!

Ratigans are feared even in Hell for they can be devastating. The Fish Burner tossed and turned around in his holding cell writhing in agony at the multitudinous little bites. He was a mass of pain, he had whole pieces of his red scaly flesh missing now. His formally superb wings were in ragged tatters. Finally, he somehow managed to free himself and got them to scatter from the cell. His bitten dragon arms and body didn't even remind him of his former self.

He heard a clapping. Turning he saw an angel sitting Indian-style Ro legged, the angel was dressed all in white with fluffy white majestic wings. At first glance, Asag wondered why one of Heaven's own would be in Hell's prison, then he saw the face. That face had sad eyes that had lived through the worst atrocities man could imagine, and creator of more than he could ever fathom.

"Lucifer, I pledged my life to you. I was your number one."

"YOU WERE NEVER MY NUMBER ONE ANYTHING YOU FUCKING PATHETIC SHIT!" In an instant Lucifer was on him with spittle flying from his fangs yelling into his bitten-up face. He held his face in the air mashed against the stony walls before letting him fall in a clump of red flesh. "Placeholder at best, but I did want you to know that your incompetence was expected and now we've put something in motion that will begin End of Days on earth."

Lucifer's eyes boiled as Mical's did. The Morning Star's white robe and fluffy white wings started to peel away like a burn victim's skin. Even though he was in human form at the moment the rape, sodomy, torture and lamentation that comprised his true form started to show itself slowly until he was himself again. The Fish Burner could barely look at his master, his eyes were filled with vile maggots and the ratigans had taken their toll.

"Why, oh Lord, are you doing this?" Asag could barely speak, greasy black smoke came from deep within his long throat.

The Devil began to grow and grow, his disgusting form was massive. People's faces could be made out quite clearly under his rotting, crusty skin. The people trapped inside him screamed and begged and gagged as cock was crammed into their throats and asses. Fingers crawled just under the surface of the Morning Star tearing vaginas in half as if gutting a fish, penises were bitten off or chewed up. Lucifer was the living pallet of all despicably sinister art. The look in his eyes was not pain, or lust, or pride, or any sin at all, it was everything at once and more... There were evils in him that were known nowhere else in the Infinite. He was a living, breathing repository of all that was awful.

Lucifer held up one of his gnarled claws protruding out of what looked like a stick for an arm all charred and scrawny. He smiled as he examined it. Then, with a slow, decisive swipe he slit Asag from his throat to his genitals. The Fish Burner screamed as only dragons can. His entrails spilled out onto the cold, vomit-soaked floor. Lucifer then wrapped his clawed hands around some exposed links of Asag's bowels and then squeezed. There were no words for the pain the Fish Burner was feeling. He was learning that even though he was the Anti-Christ-In-Waiting, he had much to learn about this low, clammy place.

"Things are best like this," Lucifer winked at the injured Anti-Christ. "Things find a way of working themselves out. You'll soon see."

TWELVE

The screams rose in volume the closer the boat got to the lit opening at the end of the ride. The bars holding people in place released their protective embrace and the water got choppy rising and falling.

It's a small world after all, it's a small world after all, it's a small, small world...

The machines ground to a halt. The boats bumped into one another as the ride operators left their post for the afterlife. The foursome got out and had to maneuver over the water to try to escape. The golden falcons were massive.

"What's going on?" David shouted over the din of the battle raging just yards from where they stood.

"Armageddon, four horseman and shit," said an Indian lady in a feathered headdress. "We thought it was part of the parade but then she pointed to her husband whose face was clawed up sinking slowly into shock.

"D'mon, can you stop this?" Jessica whispered, trying her best to hold it together.

"This isn't right, this shouldn't be happening," D'mon was desperately thinking what to do.

"Oh, but it is happening, demon spawn," Mical swooped in and landed near the three and a half humans. "You over stayed your welcome and strayed from the path you were given. Don't act like you didn't cause all of this." He swung his arms up to show the scenes of carnage and misery going on all around them. There was blood, screams, sulfur and destruction everywhere. Chrissy quivered as she saw the end of people's lives in their transformation into salt. "You're going home, demon."

"I'm here with Hell's blessing."

David and Chrissy stepped away in shock and terror. That was a fucked-up sentence to say to a fucking ass kicking crazy as fuck angel thing!

"Take off that flesh façade demon." The Archangel left his flaming sword hung suspended in mid-air and reached for the demon's face. D'mon twisted from his grasp and swung his right hand that landed on the angel's chest plate pushing him back. Feathers came loose as he was hurdled ten feet back almost hitting the ground but catching himself in mid-air. This was the first time in millennia that Mical had started to laugh.

"I am human now. I belong here. I have a soul." David and Chrissy held onto Jessica and watched this from behind. "I have a family and I wish to stay with them. Where is your compassion?"

"That's the other angel."

"Jessica do something, you're still kind of a demon right?"

"You have her soul. Those beings around you are nothing, I tire of this." Mical took the sword from its floating sheath of air and split it into two flaming swords and twirled them around. Damien-ki Zakire Monteloflobe stood his ground in a fighting stance, his knuckles cracked ominously as he balled his fists up tightly.

"One of the few things in the universe that can kill an Angel is this." The former demon's dark brown fleshy hands tore open with a red hue. D'mon let out a blood curdling scream. Demon claws with dark black nails sprouted from his hands, "You and me Mical, it ends now. I am no pushover demon. I am the taker of souls, scourge of humanity. I will not go down easily."

David and Chrissy screamed out in pain as a spear carved its way through them both with the effort of a hot knife through butter. With all eyes on Mical, zadZiel was able to swoop in from behind and slice them both. D'mon turned to witness the last moments of his new friend's lives ending. This was the second time Mical had laughed in millennia. What a wonderful day.

"Nooo!" D'mon yelled.

zadZiel knelt beside Chrissy and with a smile said. "Your child is not lost, it will be reborn. God is merciful." Chrissy with her dying breath reached up and stabbed zadZiel under the jaw with a steel shard of rollercoaster scaffolding that had been scattered amongst the debris. White light shone from the angel's mouth where the metal pierced thru. zadZiel gurled unable to speak.

"Fuck you, motherfucker," She said, then Chrissy was gone.

"Merciful?" D'mon leapt with demon hind legs that ripped through his human flesh. He landed on zadZiel and tore at him vigorously. D'mon's eye were black again and glowing with the red light of Hell within. D'mon gritted his teeth as the transformation set in. Horns grew from his forehead and a lashing tail sprouted from his ass. D'mon climbed like a panther onto one of the bastard cherubs, ripping, tearing, and punching at him. zadZiel dropped his spear as the fight drained from his body. White light poured thru every wound D'mon inflicted on the Archangel. Finally, D'mon palmed zadZiel's pale face and gripped with his entire demon might ripping his face off and tossing the flesh aside. A blinding beam of light shone out from where there was no longer a face. D'mon got off of the angelic corpse trying to see where Mical was.

"Demon, what is so special about this one?" The voice came from everywhere.

D'mon pointed to the faceless Archangel.

"That's gonna be you soon enough, Michael."

"It is pronounced Mical."

"Suck my big, black fuckin' Demon dick, you asshole!" D'mon raised his arms in the air, turning slowly as he heard Jessica's muffled cries. When he turned around he saw her held high up in the air by God's number one, both of the red-haired writer's little arms lost in his one large left hand. She wriggled and screamed from far above. "Put on the chains, boy." Mical took solid gold shackles and tossed them down to D'mon to lock his wrists with. As the demon moved away from the faceless skull, light beamed upward and now shone through the hole on zadZiel's missing face.

"You got me. Stop all this and let her go. Show that Godly mercy."

"I love you, D'mon Rhodes! Bestseller or not you're my dream come true!" the petite writer confessed.

"Wrong Angel, Godly Mercy, that's zadZiel whom you disfigured and murdered. I'm not that angel." He dropped Jessica and she fell. Upon hitting the pavement in front of a cotton candy stand a grouping of golden falcons bore down on her in a swarm of pecking and tearing. Blood and bits were flung in all directions. D'mon's eyes widened in panic! Jessica's screams sent lightening thru D'mon's veins. The Hellfire within him burned fiercely, his rail whipped and cracked. Blood oozed from the soulless writer and the demon was deflated. D'mon hung his head in shame. He fell to his knees. To his right were the speared dead bodies of the friends that had accepted him, and to the left was his one true love. His only love and compassion in an empty evil world. All around was a sideshow of terror and Hell, salt and agony. He knew he had done this, Damien-ki Zakire Monteloflobe did all this because he was bored. D'mon locked himself into Mical's golden bonds.

Mical pulled D'mon up to face level, with its arms still pinned behind him by the ethereal chains. Damien-ki Zakire Monteloflobe was defeated, physically and emotionally. The last remaining human flesh fell aside, and he stood there simply a captured Soul

Trader. The best and most cunning that Hell had to offer, and he was snatched like a common thug.

"zadZiel please bring the thetans back to Glory, for now bliss and Shangri-la is thier's to enjoy," Mical waited patiently for the once seemingly dead Archangel to piece himself back together. "I'll join you after I drop this package off in Hell." Mical stared at D'mon, then he took a good look around at the golden falcons swarming over the happiest place on Earth. "Your nightmare has just begun."

"One thing before I go, demon," zadZiel leaned towards the now fully exposed demon, "You did not just lose your mate today. She was with child and I believe it was yours."

D'mon's eyes flashed with rage, but subsided thinking better of any futile ranting. He looked at the round skull showing beaming with light where zadZiel's missing face had been. D'mon then sighed and looked to where his face was on the ground.

"Don't forget to pick up your face."

Then it was over. The golden spindles surrounding the entrances and exits were opened. Mical waved his hands and the Earth started to crack and crumble. The concrete started to shift rip apart. Hell fire breathed forth from the depths bellow. Mical soared high into the blue sky and then dove down, down into the flames emanating from the gaping hole at the center of the once Happiest Place on Earth.

Mical soared lower and lower into fire and brimstone, he brought two golden falcons with him to drag D'mon by his chains through the passageways beyond Earth's Hell. Their plummet was deep and vile during which cheers and hoots were heard from those in charge of Hell and the citizens therein. President Duulexebub cheered with his whores at his side on the balcony of the giant perpetually penetrating cock-office. Pee Wee and countless others employed in Hell watched this would-be Satanic poser fall on his ass. Cruz the Scarfel locked eyes with D'mon from afar then looked away abashed. From with the wormholes that lead to the Lake of Fire, the domain of Lucifer, the Morning Star personally watched the return of his AWOL Soul Trader. The space between the worlds was not enough to contain the wrath that Lucifer was feeling. His rape-covered physique boiled over with anal fistings and hot poker dildos plunged into rectums and throats. The dark, chilling laughter of the Morning Star could be heard from one side of the Infernal realm to the other.

"Brother, I have brought you a present," the Archangel Mical's voice echoed as loudly as his brother's laughter.

In the wake of Mical's reckoning was left an ashy and salted family amusement park. All bodies were blowing in white clusters of dust and salt. To the outside world looking in, there was or could have been some bizarre natural disaster. Or maybe it was a nuclear attack? Iran? Japan? Cuba? The insurance companies were going to have a field day with this fiasco. Ohhhh, the ramifications of angels and demons and Gods and devils doing horrendous things to a planet full of primitive savages made for great comedy and folly. Blame it on the space aliens. The wild assertions of such devout believers with absurd levels of blind asinine faith would not be believed by anybody sane.

It was winter in the middle of summer. The soot danced in the air, a vile and toxic snowstorm raged. Rides were covered in the disfigured, dismembered bodies of innocent people guilty of nothing except being sheep in a universe run by wolves. This was a veritable Hiroshima. The aftermath and desolation looked like an atom bomb had gone off, but there was no atom bomb. However, there was something much worse… an Archangel. Mical had lain waist to Disneyland. What a fucking celestial douche-bag. Only God's best warrior, His best champion would Pearl Harbor the happiest place on Earth. Prick.

Under one white clump of salt something stirred. All living

beings were now dead, but one moved. Jessica crawled out from the white storm of ash and Heavenly char. She was in bits and pieces and her heart had stopped beating but she crawled. Her heart wasn't required to pump blood because she did not have a soul of her own to propel her. She was clay, dead tissue. She was a tangible shade at best and she had lost so much. The writer could not see as her beautiful eyes were scorched and black, her vision fried away by Mical's heat. The red locks that once flowed around her pretty pale face were now blackened and full of blood, both hers and victims that had been destroyed in her proximity. Jessica Ro was as destroyed as this entire amusement park, but her emptiness kept her here. Confusion ravaged her insides. *'Where was D'mon? Did he escape? Did they kill him? Is he in some unthinkable Hell paying for helping me?'* She thought. The lonely writer started to cry. She screamed at Heaven, but her tears quickly ran out. D'mon! She was as lost now as she had been seven days ago. He giveth and He taketh away. No fucking shit. Fucker.

A hand reached out to her, she took it. It was Henry the slack-jawed dumpy guy from the Garden of Eden Nudist resort deep within the Mount Baldy Mountains. Behind him was a waiting Nudicopter with Evelyn waving sadly from the cockpit.

Henry helped the limping bloody heap of a girl into the helicopter. She could barely stand but he was strong, and she was little. Carrying her was easy enough for the handyman. Evelyn greeted her and already knew the deal. Nakey was curled up in her lap in the copter. Evelyn was no fool, she saw what bad shape Jessica was in. It was going to take more than some bandages and Tylenol and chicken soup to fix her up. The helicopter immediately lifted off. Jessica just kept nonsensically repeating D'mon's name with a weak and raspy voice; she was delusional at best, which was an ironic Godsend, because if she was firing on all thrusters she would be hysterical if she understood the severity of the situation.

"Knocked you up and left town, eh? Those bad boys will getcha everytime."

THIRTEEN

Two guards, each with two heads and barbed tails walked down the long hallway leading to the off-limits prisoner holding area. It was dark and damp all around them as they walked along the corridor in silence. Once they reached the end of the hall the cellblock leader was waiting for them. The shorter guard spoke up first. "We are here for the transfer of inmate number triple X, triple six, zero."

The leader of this particular wing of the prison sat back behind the glass in his one-room office. He eyed the guards intently and said, "That prisoner is awaiting transfer. We've been waiting awhile for this."

The holder looked in the direction of the cell and continued. "It's been difficult for me and my boys not to do the AC's job for him."

The leader smiled showing the one large jagged fang that hung from his reptile mouth. The guards nodded and hurried past as he buzzed them in through the main gate.

They shuffled along in silence for a while longer, passing other holding cells as they walked. All signs that life existed in the rooms were hidden from any passersby, but the guards had heard rumors of the kinds of horrors that continued to grow in these holding cells. These cells held creatures far too destructive to be seen even by the society of Hell. Most were considered to be top-secret failures of Hell, and out of all of them none had caused as much noise and problems as the one they were on a quest to recover.

Soon the guards reached a door marked XXX6660. They stopped and took a deep breath. The younger guard looked at the older one with a flash of fear on his face.

"You'll be fine." Grumbled the more experienced guard. "He's chained up and you know that. Don't be stupid."

"He was an Antichrist."

While the frightened green-skinned guard looked on, the shorter, browner-skinned one with more experience opened the panel on the side of the cell so he could he could talk through it and he began standard transfer procedures.

"Inmate number triple x, triple six, zero, Asag, the Fish Burner, you have been requested above ground by the High Council of the Under World. The current acting AC has been shown great leniency and mercy in offering you an opportunity to avoid your current imprisonment and eventual sentence of eternal misery in the bottomless pit. You are very lucky, Asag, the Fish Burner, prepare yourself for transfer."

A voice rose from deep in the holding cell. It spoke with purpose and did not stutter, "I am the Antichrist of Earth."

The guards looked at each other in shock and amazement. *The stories were true.* The smaller guard hit the iron bars with his baton and shouted, "That name is forbidden from you. It is only to be spoken of by the High Council. Do you understand?"

"It is who I am, you witless, worthless worm."

"That person does not exist in a prison. He never did. Prepare yourself now for transfer!" With those last words, the older, shorter guard motioned for the younger, taller, lankier guard to crank the lever pulling at the chains running along the side of the wall. He turned and turned the circular crank which in turn had the effect of pulling the thick chains which led to the cell taut. Once the inmate had been stretched out the guards entered the cell and bore witness to this legendary traitor in shackles and thick chains that hung him up by his arms. With his arms over his head, powerfully fastened, his body could be clearly made out by the guards as he hung nude.

He appeared quite similar to how he'd been depicted in writings and spoken about amongst hushed circles. His reddish tinted flesh was a sign of his birthright in the demon community, and overall his chiseled features and muscular physique of a dragon was undeniable. The guards walked close to the prisoner and stood directly beside him, their barbed tails wagging. As Asag's eyes adjusted to the light he saw his guards clearer now. The smaller guard was brown-skinned, leathery, and had various moles all over his body. He looked much like a human crossed with a toad. His yellow eyes showed no signs of kindness or understanding, only ages and ages of enjoying watching the torment of others. Asag was familiar with that look, he'd had it once himself.

The younger guard was taller, thinner, and looked as though he could play on Hell's own basketball team (if such a thing existed). His face and hands were a light green but with a clearer complexion. His eyes had a bright orange glow to them. Asag immediately sensed there was far less evil in him. He had not yet completely turned.

A frog-man and a toad-man he thought, how interesting. He looked at the guards and spoke, "They sent two Imps to pull me from this prison? I shall call you Toad and Frog. Where's Mical?"

"That's enough out of you!" The older Imp now known as Toad exploded. He took out his thick side stick with the glowing red tip and jammed it into the Dragon's side. He kicked and screamed as the hellfire electricity ran through his body. Frog, the younger Imp watched as his head fell back in submission. "See that, kid?" The toad-looking guard said. "That's how you keep these pieces of garbage in line."

The two guards adjusted the chains that held the demon tightly from his shackled claw-feet all the way to his shackled hands and led him through the hallways past the various guards and cell holders who always hollered and shouted their approval.

"Kill the bastard!"

"Make him suffer!"

Everyone they passed was philosophically against everything that Asag had once stood for, to fall as an Antichrist is a very horrible thing.

Once they made it to the elevator, the doors closed, and the older Imp selected the codes to their destination. They stood in silence waiting. It was a long trip with neither of the Imps enjoying being in such tight quarters with this abomination. It was intimidating even in shackles, the whole ride in the elevator Frog hoped the chains would hold. When the doors opened again a familiar sight greeted Asag, they were at The High Council of the Underworld. As mentally and physically strong as he appeared deep inside his stomach twisted into a knot.

The guards led him across the thick metal cliff that hung suspended in air leading to the center where The Council was arranged. On all sides of this metal cliff the drop was severe. They were far above the licks and fiery torment that lost human souls knew to be eternal damnation. Below him stood the reward that many a human evildoer could expect after their lives have ended on the surface. Standing at their positions in rows stacked high along the walls of the cave, were the leaders of all corners of the Underworld. Every providence and corner of Hell was represented, with the current reigning AC standing at a large elegant black podium addressing his people, if you could call them that. His back was to the recent arrivals but Asag, the Fish Burner, recognized fat little body and fluffy tiny wings beating heavily to keep it in air.

The guards walked the Dragon to the center and halted in front of their leader. Asag kept his eyes down, not wanting to see what creature of damnation would be responsible for his future. There was a brief moment of hushed silence before it spoke, and then came the all too familiar voice.

"Do you think these leaders came to see the great Fish Burner today?"

The Dragon prisoner turned his head to see his old second in command and now worst enemy as he rose in the air. Of course, they'd have promoted Ray Ma Ching once he himself had gotten banished, that lying piece of shit con-artist, Ray Ma Ching was one of the top sales people Hell had to offer. Ray wasn't the best though, Asag knew who the best had been, who was truly responsible for dooming more human fates than anyone. It had been D'mon whom he himself trained. He watched as Ray's fat little Asian Cherub body hung in mid-air showing off. *It's all just tricks.* Asag thought, tricks and gifts bestowed on the AC by 'The Prince of Darkness.' He'd seen this all before, if he was to be tormented, he didn't need the special effects. He wasn't impressed.

Ray's eyes made contact with the Dragon's for the first time as he hovered in the air shooting bolts of Hellfire Electricity out. His face was a cluster of pulsing veins which ran along his cheeks and his forehead. His skin had grown even doughier since Asag had seen him last, and when he spoke it just reminded him of everything wrong with this place. He looked away to his sides to see the two guards who stood with Hellfire electric batons ready.

"I asked you a question, do you think these leaders came to see you today?" The AC swung back and forth in the air and continued. "Do you think they came here to commend your treachery, your lies, your turning your back on your people by allowing your favorite Soul Trader to escape? No, that's not it. For what you have done, and the crimes you've committed against our society you deserve to be torn apart by a thousand ratigans!" He rolled the R making it sound much more like Rrrrrrratigans for emphasis to the audience. The Council reacted loudly for ratigans were feared in Hell even amongst these strong leaders. No one fucked with a ratigan. That surely was a punishment befitting such a traitor and everyone approved. They'd begun the gnawing at him and Ray insinuated that they should finish him. Ray Ma Ching lowered himself to the Dragon's level and got in the subdued prisoner's face.

"These great and powerful leaders have gathered to see the great hero Asag, the Fish Burner, *on his knees!*" With that comment he shot Asag's body with multiple bolts from his newly gifted powers. The pain hit Asag and was excruciating. He bucked and twisted against the chains but to no avail. The toad guard smirked and let him fall forward onto his face.

From his new position he saw through the many holes in the metal walkway and could make out the bubbling redness far below flowing over itself in excitement like lava in a volcano or a mass of fat worms. He could make out the specs that were mixed in with the redness, like ants on a pile of sugar. He knew what they were. Souls from all over the universe, and some of them were human souls. They were being tortured, raped, and molested until the potential End of Days. Another lifetime ago a large portion of these souls were brought to Hell by his top salesman, D'mon personally.

"How should the legend of Lucifer be represented here? I believe 'Hero' is the word! He is the Angel of the Lake of Fire, I say this as the most favorite angel of them all. The fact that his own brother is still respectful of the Morning Star shows how powerful our fearless leader is. And wise, let's not forget wise!" Ray Ma Ching kissed ass like a champion.

Then as if on cue, Ray was greeted by Mical who had no desire to be in this putrid land a second longer than necessary. "Once all the planets are diseased by Hell only then will the cure be enacted. It will be you Lucifer who will be taken down in chains."

"Yeah, well, fuck you."

"Clever, very clever. You are already defeated Lucifer."

"Maybe, but certainly not by you, *brother.*"

"You stopped being my brother when you rose up against the almighty God!"

"Shut up already. You are not God, and I don't have to be 'clever' with words, me shitting in your empty eye sockets will speak volumes and *that* will be clever enough. Right now, zillions of horrendous atrocities are taking place in all of creation and it's because of me! Rapists, murderers, liars, adulterers, child molesters, serial killers and more every day... I have more worshipers and Twitter followers than you'll ever have, and I'll tell you a secret, the book's not over yet. So, I'll see you in the next chapter, bitch."

Back and forth MICAL vs. LUCIFER are locked as always in eternal war.

"Keep your wretched pets on their leashes dear brother. I would have to transform Heaven into a cosmic kill shelter for your stable of unruly monsters. Love, brother, I leave you with a notion of love." Mical seemed at first glance to be a poet. Mical swiftly pulled the AWOL demon from thin air, leaving D'mon in their infernal custody stressing that it took Heaven to do what Hell couldn't.

"My job is to reward not punish."

D'mon was till locked in his golden chains. He struggled looking at his mentor, his boss, his friend who was suffering the same fate, Asag, the Fish Burner. D'mon saw beyond him an Imp looking like a Toad Man reminding him of Disney's 'Mr. Toad's Wild Ride' and what David, his friend had said forever ago. D'mon looked down to the souls in damnation. Back only a few days ago he felt differently, was proud of filling the place up, being the standout on such a successful team, in many ways he felt differently about what a human soul was now.

Knowing what D'mon knew now about these humans he couldn't help but feel sorry for the poor souls who endured this kind of fate. *What kinds of things could these people have done on the surface that would bring them this as a punishment?* he thought.

In the collecting of fresh souls, it was mostly impulse decisions that humans regretted later when it was too late. D'mon felt regret for his involvement in this cycle. Sadly, it would continue on with or without his involvement in it. As he could clearly see by Ray Ma Ching was next in charge to be worshipped as The Antichrist. Had the End of Days been called down right now so this stupid fat asshole with man-boobs would be in charge to lead Hell toward its attack and conquer Earth along whatever other conquered planets had intelligent life in the cosmos. D'mon knew that some of the High Council represented parts of the farthest reaches of the universe and past that even to the edges of Infinity.

Hellfire energy tore through him a second time raising a scream from D'mon and brought his attention back. Ray stood proudly behind him and continued, "Damein-ki, you were once one of the greatest Soul Traders of all time. You brought more souls into Hell than any anyone else. You were powerful, respected, and could have had it all. But you threw it away to live on the surface with the humans. You became a fugitive, an outlaw. You become *a traitor*."

Disruptions arose from The Council as they rumbled at his blasphemy.

"How pathetic to think that at one time you were almost considered Antichrist material, you!" Ray Ma Ching laughed at the notion and looked on at D'mon's present state. Even as he lay in pain and chains, D'mon felt pity for Ray and the whole industry. Being an AC meant so much to Ray and that was pathetic.

Asag breathed fire from his shackles at the chubby cherub but to no avail. The Fish Burner was weak, and Ray had inherited an upgrade in dark powers.

"Good luck with trying to fricassee Ray Ma Ching, fat boy," Ray squeezed out the most irritating laugh since before laughter was invented.

When D'mon was offered the role of AC he turned it down on multiple occasions, he knew that the day-to-day grind of Hell's

Admission Sales job was bad enough without needing to be in charge of motivating and leading its team. It was a dead-end position and D'mon regretted nothing that he had done in leaving this wretched place. Ray eyed this traitor of Hell up and down, before continuing.

"Lucifer, in His grand mercy, has agreed to offer you a chance to redeem yourself to this Council. All you need to do is accomplish what you used to do on a regular basis. You just need to do your job."

D'mon looked up from the metal mesh.

"No. Fuck no."

"There is something that burns brightly on the surface."

No please. Not one more soul.

"We have not had an opportunity for such power in centuries."

Please God, no.

"Lucifer has chosen you to claim it for us."

Fighting back anger, frustration, and even surprising to himself, tears, D'mon crawled to a sitting position and spoke, "Why me?"

"Because Demon, you are a Soul Trader, the best Soul Trader that ever was. You tried to run from your lot in life once, Dameinki, but it's time you owned up to what you are. Do not question what our Dark Lord the Morning Star has laid out for you. You have been given the opportunity of having your life spared in exchange for this essence. Just do your job and don't fuck it up.

"No more souls. I will not collect another soul."

"Well you are in luck my dear fucktard, because this is not a human soul. No, no, we all know how easily manipulated these humans are. It's not even a challenge for you anymore; all you do is study up on your sales material and then give it what it wants. The buzzwords, the catch phrases, these people are all the same, offer it a car, or a house, or the love of its favorite mate. Who cares? Time after time, you would just bring its soul back to us and you were rewarded. This is different."

D'mon and Ray looked at each other with unbridled hatred.

"Shortly the Archangel Mical will be bound to Earth by magic. The process has been put in place and with your history we thought you might want to kill him in the name of Hell."

"If you are so powerful why don't you go kill him yourself, you little limp-dicked asshole?" Asag hollered.

Ignoring Asag, Ray continued, "but if you fail, first we'll dig that cunt's soul out from your gut. Don't think we forgot about your thievery. You think you're smarter than Hell? In some ways this Angel essence is more power than a soul because it can breed new life. I was birthed from just his tears remember? Then after we've removed the soul from you, you will be cast immediately into the bottomless pit with no vacations. Along your way to the pit you may be meeting various ratigans on the way down. Pass or fail either way this Council will be pleased."

From his knees D'mon scanned The Council of the Underworld and saw that it still looked much the same as he'd remembered: Various fucktards that resembled insects and creatures he had seen from the surface. There were monsters resembling large snakes, scorpions, spiders, hundred-legged worms, and other unfriendly evil whose presence would make the most stalwart human squirm. If a human imagines it or fears it, it comes to pass somehow, living and breathing here, Lucifer has seen to that. These minions of Hell all chattered their teeth and stomped their feet loudly awaiting his answer. Below them all the lifeblood of Hell bubbled up and continued to roll over itself in anticipation. He knew Lucifer waited.

It wasn't much of a choice. D'mon nodded, at least pleased to not be willed to harm more souls.

"As for why I don't go do it myself, first of all I am needed here to lead these noble minions of Lucifer properly, something you couldn't do, obviously. Also, preparations are needed. You see, my vehicle for rebirth is being formed now. The Antichrist shall be born shortly on Earth, of a soulless zombie shell of a woman named Jessica and the seed of a pure *demon or should I say D'mon* should do the trick."

"Indeed," Lucifer bellowed, "Everything always works out in the end. The act was consummated on the Earthly plane, not born of Heaven nor Hell and yet born of love, and that's well, lovely."

"Once that little crossbreed fucker turns eighteen," Ray said letting his stubby little hands ripple with hellfire energy. "I get the driver's seat and I'll begin my very own Hell on Earth!"

TIM CHIZMAR

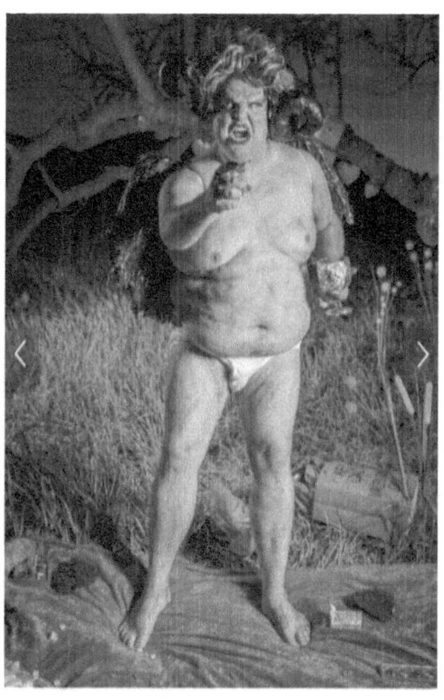

Photo Credit: Gavin White & Laura Raczka, Evil Cupid
Series

After graduating from *Edinboro University of Pennsylvania* with his bachelor's degree in Communications, and obtaining his Master's Degree in Demonology from *Miskotonic University*, Tim Chizmar has written for various magazines, newspapers and websites including *Fangoria*, *First Comics News*, *Girls and Corpses*, and many others. He has sold short stories to such collections as *Chicken Soup for the Soul* and has written various screenplays for Hollywood production companies. Tim has been a proud member of various writers' organizations including the Los Angeles Chapter of the prestigious *Horror Writers Association.*

Aside from the darker topics, it has not all been a career of terror as his lighter credits to date include *ABC, FOX, Showtime, Playboy, NBC, The Hallmark Channel*, and many more. He has produced various pilots including in 2010 he developed a comedy/action series for *CMT* with wrestling superstar Rob Van Dam. As a headlining comedian Tim was a favorite at *The World-Famous Hollywood IMPROV, The Jon Lovitz Comedy Club*, has toured all over the world playing sold-out casinos, clubs and colleges. To date he has worked with such standup legends as Jeff Foxworthy, Gabriel Iglesias, Jon Lovitz, Daniel Tosh, and many others.

When he's not inspiring fellow writers by being on various panels such as *San Diego Comic-Con, WonderCon, Scare LA,* or speaking at Hollywood Success events, he's constantly working on his next project. Because for Tim Chizmar... There's always a next project! After Tim had been successful enough to become a regular at red carpet premieres, he left all the glitz and glam behind in early 2017 for the mountains of Idaho as he completed this book. He always looks forward to having frank, honest, and engaging discussions on the business of the writing craft with his fellow writers. Tim's advice to young writers is this…

"Be inspired. Are you alive, or are you just breathing?"

twitter.com/TimChizmar

instagram.com/timchizmar

amazon.com/author/timchizmar